LOVE-BLOCKED

MESSY HEARTS #5

CHARITY PARKERSON

—Warning: This book is intended for readers over the age of 18.

Copyright © 2020 Charity Parkerson
Editor: BZ Hercules & Consultants
Photographer: Dan Skinner
ISBN: 978-1-946099-70-9
All rights reserved.

INTRODUCTION

When Derreck's old flame gains a whole new outlook, Derreck will need to find himself if he hopes to win him back.

There was a time when Jett had issues. He didn't respect himself and didn't care if anyone else treated him the way he deserves. Age and counseling have changed all that. Jett has grown some backbone and self-respect. That's exactly why his ex has no clue how to handle him now.

Derreck has dated a lot of men in his life. He's loved and lost like everyone else, but he's never lost anyone like Jett. He can't get past the emptiness. When he had his shot with Jett, Derreck didn't treat

Jett as the blessing he should have. Now Jett is strong and independent. He doesn't need Derreck at all. Derreck has never wanted anyone more. But Derreck isn't the only one with Jett in his sights, and Derreck no longer knows if that's a good or a bad thing.

If there's any shot of making things work with Jett, Derreck will have to face at least one truth about himself: he wants more than he realized the first time around. It's a good thing someone else sees Jett and Derreck for who they really are, and he knows exactly what they need—him.

ONE

"Do you remember the first time I saw you?"

"How could I forget?"

Derreck acted as if Jett hadn't responded. "You were chained to Antonio's bed." Derreck's gaze slid down Jett's body. "Wearing nothing but a collar. There wasn't an ounce of shame written on your face as I stared at you." Derreck sucked in a ragged-sounding breath, as if the memory had him hard. "Fucking beautiful."

"Can I buy you a drink?"

Jett's gaze moved to the man hovering over his table. He was probably thirty. Nice looking. Dark hair and light blue eyes. Still, Jett wasn't interested. "I don't drink but thank you."

A practiced smile lit the man's features. "It doesn't have to be alcohol."

Jett bit back a grin. "I'm working."

The man's gaze moved toward the window Jett had been staring out while lost in memories of loving Derreck... again. "Gazing out the window is considered working for you?"

"Yes."

The man's eyes flashed with humor. "Hmmm. Intriguing. Maybe a raincheck, then."

"Maybe," Jett said, allowing his usual flirtatious nature to peek through.

The guy moved along, no worse for the swing and miss.

Jett went back to staring out the window. He hated when his job brought him here and left him watching the place where he had once lost everything. He wondered if Derreck was inside, working Luna Casino's west location. Jett would likely never know. He hadn't stepped foot inside the place since Derreck broke them. It had been Lombardi High-roller Casino back then, back when Antonio Lombardi owned the place. Now Antonio lived in Phoenix with his husband. Lombardi had changed names and the world kept turning. Nothing ever stayed the same.

The man allegedly committing insurance fraud that Jett had been hired to watch strolled from the casino to his car. Not a limp in sight. A smile tugged at Jett's lips as he fired his camera to life, recording the moment. In some cases, his job was an asshole's employment. Jett had always been shameless and being an investigator for an insurance company's fraud division paid decent enough. It was easy work. Quiet. Jett had come to appreciate the silence since he had spiraled out of control almost a year ago. Jett didn't like to think about those days. Being here, this close to Derreck, left him little choice. His mind couldn't focus on anything else.

With a few seconds of video footage under his belt, and the subject of his inquiry getting away, Jett quickly slipped from the booth. His car was parked nearby. If he hurried, he could follow the guy to his next stop. Jett found his path blocked by a familiar tank-sized chest. Despite knowing it was Derreck blocking his path, Jett decided not to acknowledge his recognition.

"Excuse me." Jett tried stepping around him without further incident.

Derreck stepped sideways, keeping his path blocked. "Hey, Jett."

Jett took a bracing breath and lifted his chin. At

the first glimpse of Derreck's odd-colored amber eyes, Jett's heart hurt, his knees weakened, and his resolve doubled. "Excuse me. I'm kind of in a hurry." He tried once again to push his way past Derreck.

Derreck didn't budge. "It's been a while."

"I really have to go."

"Jett, I—"

"He says he needs to go."

Jett's gaze shot over his shoulder. The man who had offered him a drink earlier stared at Derreck with cold eyes—like Derreck wasn't twice his size.

"You should mind your business."

The new arrival obviously had no fear. He didn't back down. "And you obviously can't hear. When a man says, 'excuse me,' you move."

While the pair were focused on each other, Jett scurried around Derreck and out the door. Unfortunately, he had lost the man he needed to follow. Jett pulled out his phone and searched for the guy's address. He would cruise by and see if he spotted anything. If the guy wasn't home, then now was the perfect time to get some exterior shots of his house. Steep stairs and whatnot.

"Are you okay?" Jett spun as the words washed over him. His heart raced into his throat. His savior from inside stood with his hands clasped behind his back and keeping his distance. He eyed the way Jett patted his chest, trying to slow his racing heart. "Apologies. I didn't mean to startle you."

A nervous chuckle escaped Jett. "No. It's fine. I was lost in thought and didn't hear you coming." He tried to return some normalcy to the moment. "Thank you for your help earlier. I'm Jett, by the way."

The man's sexy, full lips quirked in one corner. "Kirill." There was a definite Russian accent that made an appearance as Kirill gave his name.

Jett's smile grew. "I hear that accent you've either grown out of or you're trying to hide."

Kirill's half smile exploded into a full grin. "Not hiding. Just Americanized after so many years on this soil. But Mother Russia will always be home," he tacked on with an extremely thick accent and a smile.

Wow. He really was pretty hot, and he had stood up for Jett when Derreck had materialized from nowhere. Derreck. Damn. He still looked beautiful too. Jett forced himself to shut down that line of thought. He glanced at his phone. The address he had been searching was over an hour's drive away. He checked the time before focusing on Kirill again. "As I said earlier, I don't drink, but maybe I could buy you one. If you're not busy, that is. As a way of thanking you for your help." His gaze slid past Kirill to the bar where he had left Derreck behind. "And maybe not here."

"I will keep you safe if you'd like to stay."

Jett tried for a smile. "My physical safety isn't in any danger. That was my ex."

Kirill's eyebrows rose. "Oh. Well, that certainly explains his rage. I can't say I wouldn't be beating my chest too, if I lost someone like you."

A laugh burst from Jett. Charming men had always been his weakness. Unfortunately, charmer usually equaled cheater. Seduction was a game some men couldn't stop playing. No matter who it hurt.

Kirill nodded toward the Luna across the street. "If you'd like, we could head to the Luna instead."

Jett did his best not to flinch. It was like there was no escaping Derreck today. "A hotel? I think I'll pass. I'm not that easy."

Laughter swam in Kirill's eyes. "If only I was that bold. How about this? How about I walk you to your car and kiss your cheek? I'll flatter you along the way by telling you how incredibly handsome you are. We can part ways with both of us feeling like we had a charming first date."

Seriously, Jett couldn't stop smiling. This guy was something else. "First date, huh?"

Kirill nodded. "When you're ready for our second date, come to either Luna location, and ask for me. I'm the general manager. They'll know how to find me."

The urge to burst into a fit of uncontrollable laughter nearly felled Jett. It seemed he had a thing for attracting Derreck's bosses. Instead of humiliating himself, Jett motioned toward his car. It was a silver Camry that looked like a million others. Jett needed to blend in while following people. "I'm right here. If you'd like, we can walk slow. I'd hate for you to feel our date was rushed."

The humor etched in Kirill's features made Jett glad he hadn't refused to speak to the man. He looked nice. Jett imagined he could and did have anyone he wanted. Despite Kirill's many qualities, Jett didn't plan to seek out that second date. He was better single. There was no one out there worth giving up his peace. Jett would know. He had looked.

"DID YOU REALLY COME HERE TO BEG NINO TO *take you back after sleeping with me?*"

Jett didn't look the least bit guilty. He lifted one delicate shoulder in a careless shrug. "You don't really want me. You just don't want Nino to be with me."

Derreck's temper snapped. He was fucking enraged at the idea of Jett running back to Antonio. Jett was his. His fist shot out, connecting with the wall beside Jett's head. Jett didn't as much as flinch as Derreck's knuckles split. Nothing could have spoken louder to him, cutting through his rage more than Jett's accepting expression. He expected Derreck would hit him—like everyone did. Derreck's hands shook as he cupped Jett's face. He shuffled closer, crowding Jett's space.

"How can you not see that I'm the one who wants you for you? No games. No chains or collars. I just want the real you. The you that you keep hidden. I'm not afraid of the damage everyone else has caused."

A tear spilled from Jett's lashes. "You don't want that." Jett's voice was barely a whisper.

"Derreck. Table ten needs you to count them out."

Derreck blinked, coming back to reality as the memory disappeared. He nodded the waitress's way and got back to work. Deep in his chest, Derreck ached. He still had an hour left on the clock. All he could think about was watching Kirill walking away with Jett. From his spot in the bar, he hadn't been able to see where they had gone. It had taken every ounce of his strength to grab a seat, order his lunch, and pretend nothing happened. Goddamn. Jett looked good. Truthfully, he probably looked exactly the same, but Derreck hadn't seen him in so long. Jett's beauty had sucker punched him. He was unlike anyone else. His sweet brown eyes screamed innocence, but his full lips begged for the dirtiest acts. When he focused on men, Jett made them weak. Derreck couldn't blame Kirill for pursuing him.

Bitterness welled in Derreck's throat. His gaze slid Kirill's way. When Derreck's best friend Antonio had sold the hotel casino to the owners of Luna, he had worked a deal for Derreck. On paper, the offer sounded amazing. They had to keep Derreck in his position as pit boss at a considerably higher pay than he had previously made. Or they had to offer him a minimum of two hundred thousand in severance pay. They had easily agreed to Antonio's terms, which should have been the first red flag. No one had thought about them making his life hell, so he willingly left, forfeiting his severance deal. That was where Kirill came in.

The day after Antonio's departure, Kirill had swept

into the casino. Things changed immediately. No longer was Derreck's job the happy home it had once been. Kirill watched and criticized his every move. Whereas Antonio had been warm and welcoming, Kirill was cold and calculating. The bastard had been all smiles while chatting with Jett. Goddamn. It was like Derreck was cursed when it came to Jett. First, Antonio had swept Jett off his feet while Derreck watched. Now, it seemed, Kirill would do the same. Derreck was just some guy. He was the one who loved Jett, but he was just some guy, nonetheless. Jett could have anyone.

"Do you want to talk about the angry looks you've been shooting my way all afternoon?"

Derreck kept his expression blank by force of will alone as Kirill materialized beside him. He wouldn't give Kirill the pleasure of letting the man know he had gotten under Derreck's skin with Jett. "There's nothing to talk about. I'm sure I haven't looked your way all day."

The deep satisfaction that settled into Kirill's features had Derreck mentally holding himself back. "Ah. You are angry over Jett."

Damn. Derreck really wanted to punch him in the throat. He said Jett's name with the perfect amount of caress—like he had already tasted him.

"Why would I be angry about Jett? That boy is punishment enough all by himself. He'll make you sorry for chasing him."

Kirill grunted. "That's funny. I found him lovely. He's gorgeous and has a good job. I would think he'd be a true prize for anyone strong enough to catch him."

Derreck ground his back teeth to a pulp at the subtle jibe. "Good luck to you, then."

For a moment, Kirill's unusually light blue eyes seemed to stare into Derreck's soul. When he spoke, he sounded entirely too knowing for Derreck's peace of mind. "I find it odd that you act as if you don't want him. Yet you refused to move from his path when he showed no interest in you."

"We have history and I had something I needed to say. He didn't want to hear it. That's not interest. That's a stalemate."

"So you don't want this," Kirill said, holding up a sheet of paper torn from a Luna notepad.

Derreck's gaze slid the page's way. "Am I supposed to know what that is?"

Kirill's lips lifted in one corner. "Jett's address and phone number."

Temptation punched Derreck so hard, his knees

weakened. "I'm sure he meant that information for you."

Kirill shrugged. "He didn't give it to me. I had a friend find out his information for me."

That was usually Derreck's move, gathering information on the sly. Longing clawed at Derreck's guts. He fought the urge to snatch the paper from Kirill's hand. Instead, he shook his head. "He's been done with me for a long time. That's all you." Derreck put one foot in front of the other and forced himself to move in the opposite direction of Jett's address. Some things people couldn't take back. Derreck kissing Antonio, after promising his heart to Jett, was one of those things.

TWO

As hard as Jett tried not thinking about Derreck, he couldn't stop. Damn, he swore he could still smell Derreck's cologne lingering on his clothes, even though they hadn't touched—like it had when they were together. He loved the way Derreck smelled—spicy and sweet. Jett missed burying his face in the crook of Derreck's neck and inhaling as Derreck's huge arms closed around him. He could still feel the warmth of Derreck's chest. No one had hugged him since Derreck. It was such an odd realization to hit from nowhere.

Jett stared at where the corner of his living room met the ceiling while lost in thought. Everything in life had a final time that no one realized was the last. In hindsight, Jett recognized he should have known his relationship with Derreck didn't have a shot. He should have treated every touch like it would be the last. Hope was funny like that, though. He hadn't wanted to believe they would end. Now look at him. Forever single. It was for the best.

Jett's cellphone rang, pulling him from his thoughts. He was off the clock, so he had no idea who would be calling. He didn't have friends anymore. It was an unknown caller, but the area code was local. With a shrug, Jett answered. If it was a telemarketer, he could block their number.

"Hello?"

"I'm not a stalker," a voice said quick—like they thought Jett might hang up.

"Well, I mean, I don't know who you are, so it's kind of hard to call you a liar, but that does sort of sound like something a stalker would say."

A smooth-sounding chuckle caressed Jett's ear. "It's Kirill."

"Oh." Jett didn't know what else to say. The man magically finding his number did seem a bit stalker-ish.

Thankfully, Kirill cleared the matter up immediately. "It turns out a lot of people know you around here. Did you really used to date the old owner?"

A chuckle slipped from Jett. "Scandal, I know. I dated a very rich man who's more than twenty years older than me. Surely I must be a gold digger."

"That's not at all what I meant," Kirill said, sounding slightly offended. "Antonio Lombardi is damn sexy. I want to know more."

Jett shook his head. A smile tugged at his lips. "So who's the gossip around the casino? They're giving out my number to random strangers."

An offended huff sounded through the phone. "Not only am I not a stranger, I also lied. I told the receptionist here that we were friends and I lost all my contacts in my phone. I might have gone on to say we have a date that I'd be late for, and I had no way to contact you to let you know."

"Wow, and Coral just handed my number to you."

"It's a plausible story," Kirill said, as if Jett's statement had been Jett questioning his honesty. "And I'm hoping it's a story I can make somewhat true. Have dinner with me tomorrow night."

Jett bit his bottom lip, trying to stop the out-of-control smile tugging at his lips. "What happened to me coming to you at Luna when I'm ready for that second date?"

"What can I say? I'm an impatient guy who knows when someone is too good to let get away."

This one was trouble. Jett couldn't say he wasn't into that. "Well, for our first date, I got walked to my car. What did you have in mind for a second date? Do you plan to come over so you can walk me from my car to the front door for round deux? Oh, oh, what about our third date?"

"The third date is when I ask you to finally, *finally* put me out of my misery and kiss me."

Jett covered his eyes. His cheeks ached. This was so ridiculous. "Maybe we could try a real date tomorrow night instead. Then, possibly, I won't make you wait until a third date for that kiss. Perhaps."

"I know you don't like this place, but would you be willing to meet me at work? I don't get off until seven."

Part of Jett wanted to say no, but he couldn't. He was bigger than refusing to go to Kirill's workplace because his ex might be there. "That's fine."

"Fantastic." There was so much breathless triumph in that one word that Jett blushed. "I guess I'll see you then."

Jett cleared his throat. "It seems so."

"Goodnight, gorgeous."

"Goodnight." Jett covered his eyes again as he

disconnected the call. He couldn't believe he had accepted a date with Derreck's boss. That felt like something bound to bite his ass. With a sigh, Jett tossed his phone aside. Their date didn't have to be serious. Jett wouldn't let it be. He was strong. Independent. Jett didn't need anyone. They would have dinner. He would split the check. That was it. No big deal. Jett could handle one date. Maybe.

THE APARTMENT COMPLEX LISTED ONLINE AS Jett's current address was a nice place. Each unit had a garage and looked well-maintained. Kirill had mentioned Jett had a good job now. Curiosity ate Derreck alive. He wanted to hear all about what Jett had been doing since their split. Unfortunately, he didn't think Jett would be willing to shoot the shit, even if he answered the door. That didn't stop Derreck from heading for the door.

He had no idea what he was doing here. After Derreck had made the worst decision of his life and kissed Antonio, Jett had pulled a Houdini like Derreck had never seen. Days after his calls went unanswered, Jett's number went inactive. He had been staying with Derreck, but that hadn't stopped

Jett from never returning for his things. In fact, Derreck still had everything Jett had left behind. Derreck had been tempted to bring everything tonight, but he wasn't one hundred percent certain that Jett actually lived here. It was entirely possible this was just his last known address or Jett lived with another man. A thousand things could go wrong once Derreck knocked on the door. That knowledge didn't stop his knuckles from landing.

To Derreck's surprise, the door swung wide. Jett froze, as if he never expected to find Derreck on his stoop.

Derreck managed a small smile. "I can't believe you answered." Derreck hadn't meant to say that, but shock took hold of his tongue. "I really thought you would see me through the peephole and pretend you weren't home."

Jett looked like he was contemplating shutting the door in Derreck's face. "Honestly, I didn't look. I'm expecting a food delivery. But, goddamn. Is Coral giving my information to everyone today?"

Derreck's forehead furrowed. "I don't know what Coral has to do with anything. I searched your name online and this address popped up."

Jett's expression didn't turn any more welcoming at the confession. "What are you doing here?"

"You wouldn't let me talk to you today."

A deep line appeared between Jett's eyebrows. "So you decided to hunt me down?"

Derreck fought an irritated growl. "You've never given me a chance to say I'm sorry or explain."

Jett's expression cleared. "There's nothing to explain. You wanted Antonio. Nothing or no one mattered more. I get it. I was in the way and extremely disposable. Some might even say I got exactly what I deserved when you kissed him. After all, I slept with you while I was still dating him. We're all just big pieces of shit, trying to make it through life while carrying the burden of our mistakes. Think nothing of it. I've meant nothing to a lot of men. You're not special. There. Everything has been said."

"You are special to me." Derreck held Jett's stare, mentally daring Jett to call him a liar.

"Jett?"

Jett's gaze shot to the person saying his name behind Derreck, stealing Derreck's chance to say all the things he needed to say. "That's me."

Derreck stepped aside so Jett could accept his delivery. The familiar scent of Jett's favorite Mexican restaurant wafted over him.

The moment they were alone again, Jett's gaze

dropped to the bag before he focused on Derreck again. "You know one meal at this place is like two for me. Would you like to come in and share?"

Since Derreck recognized an olive branch when he saw one, he didn't hesitate to grab his chance. "I'd love that."

With a sharp nod, Jett took a step back and let Derreck inside. Derreck closed the door and followed Jett to the kitchen. He looked beautiful. Jett was tiny and gorgeous. Thick hair and sweet brown eyes that screamed innocence. Jett sucked people in and made them want to keep him safe. Derreck was no exception.

As Jett grabbed silverware and drinks, Derreck unpacked the bag of food. He couldn't take the silence. "I haven't eaten at this restaurant since the last time I went with you."

"That doesn't surprise me." Jett moved to Derreck's side to help him split the meal evenly. "You always thought they were inconveniently located."

Derreck snorted. "They are, but I also always sort of thought of the place as our place. It seemed wrong to go without you."

Jett flashed a laughing glance his way. Derreck's breath caught in his throat. He had missed Jett more than Jett could ever know. Jett seemed oblivious to Derreck's internal struggle. "They deliver now."

"You disappeared." God help him. Derreck couldn't hold back. He needed to talk about losing Jett.

Jett's smile fell. He looked away and settled down with his food at the small kitchen table. Jett waited until Derreck sat too before responding. "You don't know me anymore, Bear. The best thing I ever did for myself was disappear."

Derreck's throat damn near swelled closed at the sound of Jett's pet name for him, and that was before Jett's claim sank in. "I kissed Antonio in a moment of desperate panic. Did that really undo every moment we shared? We had a lot of beautiful ones."

Jett ate as if Derreck hadn't said a word. A few minutes passed before he spoke. When he did, Jett sounded completely calm—like they discussed the weather. "My dad used to beat me." Jett took another bite. His expression didn't match his confession. Jett looked serene. "My whole life, except for a few months here and there when the state would step in, I always had some sort of horrific injury. Broken arm. Smashed shoulder. I can tell you when it'll rain two days ahead of time—like I'm eighty."

"I didn't know that." Derreck didn't recognize his

own voice. He sounded hollow. He had truly believed he knew Jett better than anyone on the planet, but Derreck hadn't known that.

Jett shrugged and kept talking between bites. "At seventeen, I moved in with a guy twice my age just praying to get away, but my life was the same. When I turned nineteen, I went to work as a stripper while doing a lot more for a lot more money on the side. By the time I met Nino at twenty-one, I no longer felt anything at all. I was like a dog who was kept chained unless I was in a fight for my life for someone else's entertainment. You don't know me, Bear. So the real question is: did any of the times you claimed to love me count, since you don't even know me?"

Derreck couldn't breathe. He couldn't decide what to deal with first. It was true. He hadn't known any of those things about Jett. But Jett shouldn't know Derreck loved him either. Derreck had only said the words after Jett went to sleep each night.

When Derreck didn't respond, a sad smile touched Jett's lips. "Being with you was the first time in my life I felt safe. Protected. I cheated on someone to be with you, but you still claimed to love me—like I wasn't a horrible person. Then you kissed Nino, and everything looked clearer than ever before. It finally sank into my thick skull that I am unlovable, disposable, and live in a world filled with liars, so I had better learn how to take care of myself. Maybe it took way too many years for me to learn my lesson, but I did."

Every word Jett spoke was like punching Derreck in the throat. He didn't want to believe he hadn't known every nuance of Jett. He had lived and breathed Jett from the first time he set eyes upon him —even when he had thought there was no hope Jett would notice him. Even though Derreck hadn't once doubted he was one hundred percent responsible for destroying them, he hadn't really known anything.

Jett pointed his fork toward Derreck's plate. "Eat. I don't hate you, but if you want to hang out, then don't waste the food I gave you."

Derreck didn't pick up his fork. He couldn't tear his gaze away from Jett's accepting expression. It was obvious he fully believed no one could or would love him and that was on Derreck. That would always be a black mark on his soul.

"Nino hired me off the street," Derreck said, deciding to trust Jett with the story of his life, since Jett had done the same. No one heard this from him. Not ever. "Not only was I homeless, I barely knew how to read. No one in their right mind should've trusted me to work in a casino where tons of money filters through every day. Not only did he give me a job, he let me live in the hotel and paid for years of medical treatment I needed from living on the streets. He became my family. I could never repay Antonio for the life he's given me. Losing him to Phoenix—not Bay—hit me harder than I dreamed possible." Derreck shook his head. "I know it might sound like complete bullshit, but seriously, kissing him had nothing to do with us. No doubt it didn't feel that way when it was all said and done, but at the moment, it didn't feel like anything that could touch us. I've never been that scared of losing someone. I wasn't thinking clearly."

Jett set his hand on Derreck's forearm. He rubbed. Derreck's gaze dropped to Jett's hand. It looked so pale and delicate against Derreck's dark skin. "I know about your living on the street. I pried the story from Antonio back when I realized I was falling for you." He lightly squeezed Derreck's arm before pulling away. Jett stood and carried his plate to the sink. With his back to Derreck, Jett polished off his drink. As he set his glass in the sink, Derreck pushed to his feet. On autopilot and with his heart in control, Derreck closed the distance between them. As his body collided with Jett's, Derreck automatically dropped his mouth to Jett's shoulder. For a moment, Jett melted into his hold. Derreck's heart raced. His lips moved to Jett's throat. Jett reached up and stroked Derreck's beard before stepping sideways out of Derreck's hold.

"No, thank you." Jett didn't meet Derreck's gaze as he shot him down.

"I should go." It was Derreck's broken heart and stung pride speaking, but he couldn't stay. As much as he wanted Jett back, he was weak from too much loss. The last year had kicked his ass. He was tired. When it came to Jett, Derreck didn't know how to fight. Never had.

"You didn't touch your dinner."

Without meeting Jett's stare, Derreck flashed a smile. "Save it for lunch tomorrow. I'm sure that was your original plan. Thanks for giving me a chance to explain. I'm sorry I failed you."

"Bear," Jett said, sounding exasperated.

Derreck didn't slow on the way to the door. He understood he couldn't go back in time and make better choices. Derreck couldn't make their relationship healthy or start out on a different foot. He had fallen in love with his best friend's lover, acted on that love, and ruined everything. It didn't matter Antonio hadn't loved Jett and Derreck did.

Equally, it mattered not at all that kissing Antonio hadn't touched Derreck's heart. Derreck had destroyed them. There was no going back from that.

JETT FOUGHT THE URGE TO CHASE DERRECK TO the parking lot. The old him would have done just that—no matter the personal cost. He couldn't be that person anymore. Desperate looked ugly on everyone equally. If Derreck had really loved him, which Jett doubted since Derreck had cheated, then he had loved a version of Jett that didn't exist anymore.

The day Derreck had chosen Antonio, Jett had spent the afternoon with Antonio's man—a doctor named Bay. While Bay had been every bit as broken-hearted as Jett, he wasn't self-destructive like Jett. Instead of burning down Antonio's casino, the way Jett wanted, Bay threw himself into helping Jett. For some reason Jett couldn't explain, he had started talking and hadn't stopped. Jett told Bay everything, while carefully avoiding the fact that he had once dated Antonio. Bay had listened and then handed Jett the harshest truth: he needed professional help.

Jett needed counseling and probably meds. Bay

had gone on to reassure Jett there was no shame in reaching out rather than suffering, especially since he likely suffered PTSD from years of abuse. While Jett's first reaction had been to lash out, he hadn't. Since Bay was a doctor, nice, and extremely intelligent, Jett chose to see the man's advice as a free trip to the clinic. The next day, Jett had gone to see his primary care physician and gotten the referrals required to get the help he needed. His life had completely changed from that moment on. That didn't mean Jett had stopped loving Derreck. He hated the way Derreck visibly hurt now.

Jett paced and chewed the side of his nail. He hadn't tried dating anyone else since splitting with Derreck. Honestly, he didn't know if he was ready to return to the world of dating. Jett felt strong, but that feeling hadn't been tested. Even though he didn't want to risk his heart and sanity, Jett couldn't relax until he did something to stop the gnawing at his brain that had started the moment Derreck kissed his neck. Damn, he might not miss dating, but he missed Derreck's lips.

"Jesus, Derreck, it's ridiculous for one person to be as big as you are. You're like a tank." Jett poked Derreck's hard chest. *"Or a bear."* A smile exploded across Jett's face. *"You're my bear. Dance, Bear,"* Jett

said, climbing Derreck like a monkey until he hung from Derreck's back piggyback style.

"Oh, I'm a bear, huh? All right." Derreck backed up against the wall and moved up and down like scratching his back on a tree. "What's this clinging to me? It's sapping my strength." He dropped to one knee. In one quick motion, he flipped Jett to the floor. As proof of his strength, Derreck didn't hurt Jett at all. He controlled every move, ensuring Jett didn't feel any impact of the landing. Of course, Derreck's smile was so sexy and contagious, Jett wasn't sure he would've felt anything anyhow at the first sight of it. "I have you now," Derreck whispered as he lowered his head and swiped his lips across Jett's. He nuzzled Jett's neck. "I'll be your bear if you'll be my honey."

Jett's laughter vibrated against Derreck's skin. His chest unexpectedly tightened. He had never been this happy. Jett prayed Derreck didn't realize he was way too good for Jett. It would kill him.

Jett dug out his phone. He would let fate decide. If Derreck's number was the same, then Derreck would have his number. If not, Jett would see it as the universe slapping his hand and he wouldn't try again. He took a deep breath and started typing.

Jett: *This is my number now. You're still too big*

to be human, but don't worry. I won't tell anyone you're really a bear.

Jett's hands shook as he hit send. That was probably a good sign he made a mistake. There was no going back now. Jett stared at the phone until his eyes crossed. No response came. Jett took a deep breath and gave a sharp nod. He had his answer. There was nothing to pursue between them any longer. Jett put his phone on charge and headed for the shower. It was time to wash away the painful memories the only way he could now.

THREE

THERE WAS A TEXT IN HIS PHONE FROM JETT. Derreck didn't know where to go with that. The text had come in while Derreck was driving home last night, saving him in the moment. But now, Derreck had nothing stopping him from texting Jett back. Except Derreck wasn't so sure he should bother Jett again. Jett looked at peace. Derreck shouldn't rip that away. Only an asshole would do that.

Derreck stewed over his dilemma as he made his rounds at the casino. He caught sight of Kirill heading for the back offices. For a moment, Derreck's mind drifted in a different direction. Kirill wore jeans and a t-shirt. In the past year of working together, Derreck hadn't seen Kirill in anything other than expensive suits. Derreck told himself that was why he couldn't look away. Maybe that didn't completely explain the way his gaze dropped to Kirill's ass, but Derreck was a master of lying to himself. The thing was, Kirill was hot. It was impossible to miss.

Something stirred in the air. Chill bumps rose on Derreck's skin. He knew before he turned his head—Jett was there. It was like they were linked somehow. Derreck felt him. Jett's gaze skimmed the room. For a second, they held each other's stare before Jett turned away and headed for the front counter. A wave of something primal overcame Derreck. He had to do something. Simply walking across the room to say hi wasn't enough. He wanted to see Jett smile. Judging by watching Jett today and yesterday, Jett didn't do that much anymore.

An idea struck and Derreck headed for the door. He nearly ran in his rush to get back before he lost his chance. There was a woman who sold flowers from a cart each day. When Derreck spotted her right away, it felt like fate. He hurriedly purchased the nicest bouquet she had and rushed back inside.

Jett was still there, patiently standing with his hands clasped behind his back, as if waiting for someone.

Derreck practically leapt into Jett's space, holding out his gift. "You look like you need these."

Jett eyed the flowers like Derreck held out a snake. "Those are very pretty, but I don't want them."

Derreck eyed the bouquet. He was fairly certain there were no bugs and he didn't think Jett had any allergies. "What's wrong with them?"

"They're a guilt gift."

With a huff, Derreck dropped his arm. He didn't remember Jett being this difficult. "Are you fucking kidding me? That's not a thing."

"Of course it is," Jett said without missing a beat. "You know, it's like when you buy someone a Christmas gift, and then they rush out to get you one, even though they never planned to get you a gift. That's a perfect example of a guilt gift. Those are the worst. Who wants a present begrudgingly given? You never stopped by a flower cart when we were together, thinking you wanted to make me smile. Now you show up with flowers you never would've bought if we were still together. Those are guilt flowers. So, no thank you."

Derreck bit back a growl. "I don't know what you want from me."

"Oh, dear. Are those guilt flowers?"

Derreck's eyes fell closed at the sound of Kirill's voice.

Kirill clicked his tongue. "For shame. Are you ready to go, my dear?"

Jett flashed Derreck a pained smile before reaching for Kirill's arm. They walked away together, leaving Derreck behind with a bouquet of roses and looking like an idiot. Jett was leaving with Kirill. Fuck his life. The man was everywhere, taking everything from Derreck. Derreck pulled out his phone and called Antonio. He needed a friendly voice in his life. Everything sucked. The second Antonio's smooth Italian voice caressed his ear, Derreck didn't bother with saying hello. "Did you know guilt flowers are a thing?"

"Of course," Antonio said without missing a beat. "They're flowers you buy only because you feel guilty and not because you wanted to do something nice. Never, ever buy them. No one wants them."

Derreck's shoulders fell. "But I did just want to do something nice."

"Oh dear," Antonio said, matching Kirill's earlier tone to perfection. "Who did you try giving guilt flowers anyhow? I didn't think you had dated anyone since... wait. Did you see Jett?"

Derreck blew out a loud breath as he headed for

his office. It looked like he had some roses to liven up the place. Goddamn it. When it came to Jett, Derreck was always stupid.

"I'm taking your silence as a yes."

"Yeah," Derreck said, shutting himself inside his office. "And, as usual, I made a fucking idiot of myself."

"Where did you run into him? Vegas is a big place."

"He came into the casino."

"Hmmm," Antonio hummed, sounding irritated. "That sounds like he was looking for trouble."

Even though Antonio couldn't see him, Derreck shook his head. "No. Apparently, he was here for Kirill."

"The sexy Russian who you hate because he's ten years younger than you and is your boss now, and who I really shouldn't have called sexy? That Kirill?"

Derreck's lips stretched into a smile. He tossed the bouquet on his desk and plopped down in his chair. Derreck wished Antonio wasn't so far away. "Do you know a lot of Kirills?"

"Not really, but I hear it's a pretty common name in Russia."

An ache bloomed in Derreck's chest. He needed to think about something else. "How is your sexy doctor husband who I really shouldn't call sexy?"

"He's good. Speaking of which, and don't get your hopes up here, a clinic right outside Vegas sent him an offer."

Excitement had Derreck sitting forward in his seat. "Are you fucking kidding me? Are you saying I might get you back?"

"Well, you never lost me, but yeah. Bay is considering the offer. The only family he had here in Phoenix was his grandmother and she's gone. He still has her house to care for, but a management company could do that. We're discussing it. It's important to me that he's happy more than anything."

Derreck couldn't stop smiling. "That's amazing. What'll it take to convince Bay to take the job? Not that I'm getting my hopes up or anything."

"Of course," Antonio said with a laugh. "Honestly, we don't need the money, so it's all about the hours. He wants to only work part-time now so I'm not alone as often. If they offer the right schedule, we'll move. If not, we could end up anywhere. I'd tell him to just quit, but he has a calling. He loves helping people."

"And you love him," Derreck finished for him.

"Exactly, but still. The thought of coming back home sounds amazing to me. I guess Vegas is more in my heart than I realized."

Derreck's eyes burned. His throat swelled. "I get why you moved, though." Derreck swallowed. "If I wasn't such a dumbass..." Derreck didn't know how to finish that thought. A lot of things might be different in his life if he didn't fuck up everything he touched.

"You really loved him." Antonio sounded more thoughtful than anything. "I guess it's just weird to me that Jett is the one who stole your heart. I can think of at least five people you've dated who I thought stood a better chance, but nope."

"It's because he's a survivor. Just like me," Derreck said, explaining something he had never tried to put into words before. He kicked back and stared at the ceiling, seeing nothing, but lost in the memories of everything. "I guess... I don't know. He never looked at me and saw the homeless kid I'll always be. Jett always treated me like I was the savior and not the street trash who needed rescuing." Derreck realized how he must sound to the man who had saved him from the streets. "It's hard to explain." He didn't want to sound ungrateful or like they had a pity friendship. Jett was just different. Being with

Jett was the first time in Derreck's life he had felt like the hero. "No one needs me."

"I don't know. I've had to start setting alarms on my phone without you around, pestering me to take my meds."

A snort escaped Derreck. "You don't have to try to pander to my feelings. I know I'm a head case. It doesn't take a therapist to see I have issues. I know I'm like a stray dog that was dropped alongside a country road. It doesn't matter how many people keep taking me in, I'll never recover from that first abandonment." Damn. Derreck had talked himself right into self-discovery. With a sigh, Derreck came back to reality. "I guess I had better get back to work. Even though my boss is currently on a date with the love of my life, I'm certain he has some way of still knowing when I'm slacking."

"Huh," Antonio said, sounding thoughtful. "It's funny. Throughout this entire discussion, you never sounded jealous of Jett being on a date, yet I truly believe you are in love with him. I would kill anyone who thought to touch Bay."

Derreck paused. He gave Antonio's claim the thought it deserved. Unexpectedly, a smile curved his lips. "I guess, despite everything, I still don't believe we're over." The way he had felt as Jett arrived at the casino invaded his thoughts. Derreck's smile grew. "Maybe he hasn't fully accepted it yet, but in the end, I think he'll always belong to me."

It was possible Derreck was just completely insane. There was no reason for him to believe any of the words leaving his lips, but he did. Jett was his. Derreck wasn't intimidated by a date. He would find a way to win.

Spending time with Kirill was nice. They stayed on the strip. First, walking so close their elbows touched. Then, hand in hand. They found an outdoor cafe and enjoyed a light meal. More than once, Jett caught himself staring at Kirill's full lips. Kirill had a sexy way of unconsciously licking his bottom lip that had Jett fascinated. He was sexy. Jett got the feeling Kirill knew it too. The way his light blue eyes flashed with wickedness taunted Jett. Jett missed sex.

He didn't feel on even footing again until it grew late and they found a grassy area with park benches. They didn't sit. Instead, they talked while Jett stepped off and back on a foot-tall concrete slab and Kirill circled him like a hawk.

"What do you want most out of life?"

Jett chuckled at the question. "Going deep, huh?" Jett froze and stared at nothing in the distance as he considered Kirill's question. He didn't feel like he could answer honestly without sounding pathetic. Jett wanted to be loved. Overwhelmed with it. He craved drowning in unconditional and unwavering adoration, because he had never had that. Not once. Most people got that from their parents. Jett hadn't.

He must've taken too long. Kirill made a humming noise—like he had Jett's number. "I see you don't wish to tell me."

Against his will, Jett blushed. "I'm feeling exposed, I guess."

Kirill had a way of looking completely understanding that Jett had never seen. Kirill nodded. "Would you prefer if I go first? I want acceptance."

It was like falling forward into Kirill's eyes. Jett couldn't look away. He needed more confessions like he needed his next breath. "Does no one accept you as you are?"

"Not usually. Your turn."

Jett's heart beat a little faster. He swore he felt the sweat break out on his palms. "I want happiness."

It was only a partial truth, but Jett couldn't force his lips to shape the rest.

Kirill looked thoughtful before he bent and plucked a flower from the grass. He held it out to Jett. "You're worthy of that and more."

Jett curled his nose to hide the way Kirill's words punched him in the chest. "Is this a one-upping your rival flower?"

A sexy smile stretched Kirill's lips. He brushed the flower along Jett's cheek. "Derreck isn't my rival, so I don't have to best him. I don't compete for anyone's affection. I'm either wanted or not. Since you don't want me, you should accept this for the innocent gift that it is."

Jett took the flower from Kirill and brought it to his nose. "You shouldn't take it personally. I don't want anyone."

"Oh, now I don't believe that for a second," Kirill said as he invaded Jett's space. "When Derreck stepped into your space at that restaurant yesterday, you froze. You might have half-ass pretended to try to get around him, but you didn't mean it. Since don't strike me as the type to tolerate unwanted company, I have to assume you very much hoped he would say something that would undo whatever shitty thing he did that broke you."

A flash of irritation ran through Jett at the insinuation. "Maybe I was the one who broke us."

Kirill cocked his head to one side, as if truly considering Jett's words before waving them away. "No. He has guilt written all over him when he looks at you. You have something different in your eyes. I just haven't quite figured out what it is yet."

"It's bitterness," Jett said, refusing to let Kirill guess and psychoanalyze him.

For a moment, while standing entirely too close, Kirill stared into Jett's eyes before responding. His voice came out soft, caressing Jett's ears. "No. Maybe you are bitter, but that's not what I'm looking at right now. May I kiss you?"

Without thought, Jett snorted. "You've spent the last five minutes determined to pick apart my last relationship while determining I don't want you and now you want a kiss."

"Is that a no?"

Jett shook his head. He had no clue what to make of Kirill. "You're an odd man."

"And you're a fascinating one. Tell me what you see in Derreck."

Jett rolled his eyes. Kirill still wasn't backing away. Neither was Jett. "You've seen him."

Kirill nodded. "I have. All I see is his anger."

41

A small smile tugged at Jett's lips. "Then you're not looking. How can you miss that beard? Goddamn. It's delicious to run your fingers through. Not to mention, he's huge. Being with him was like... I had a brick wall protecting me." Jett's throat swelled on the confession. He swallowed past the pain.

Kirill's expression shifted, as if finally enlightened. "There it is. The real you. It's nice to meet you, Jett Weaver."

Jett didn't like feeling exposed. He had to make it stop. Jett did the only thing he could think to do. He kissed Kirill. At first, it was a stiff kiss—lips on lips with no heat. Then Kirill melted, and Jett did too. Damn. It was a good kiss. Skilled. Jett's heart rate kicked up and his body stirred.

"You are a beautiful one," Kirill said as he changed angles. By the time Kirill lifted his head to stare down at Jett, Kirill's cheeks were flushed. His eyes hooded. Jett wondered if he was one wrong move away from getting fucked in public... or one right move, depending upon how he looked at things. "I stand corrected. Maybe you want me a little after all." Even Kirill's voice had the perfect amount of lust tinting it.

Jett took a step back, immediately feeling like he

had cheated on someone who was no longer a part of his life. He couldn't meet Kirill's stare any longer. "Maybe I do."

Kirill touched Jett's jaw, forcing Jett to meet his gaze. "You have too much passion for such little self-reflection. Why has no one ever told you it's okay to want more?"

Jett had no idea what any of that meant. Honestly, he just wanted to go home. He should have accepted Derreck's guilt flowers. Likely, Derreck would never try again now. Jett swallowed past the pain that thought brought. He could admit the truth to himself as long as no one else knew. Derreck was the one for him. That was who Jett wanted to be with.

"Come on," Kirill said, taking Jett's hand. "It's time to be heard."

"What?"

Kirill ignored his question as Jett tried to keep up with Kirill's clipped pace. He had no idea what was going on, but he had a bad feeling his life had been hijacked. All Jett could do now was hang on for the ride.

Derreck was silently dying on the inside. He watched the clock, counting every second that passed while Jett was out with someone else. While, logically, he realized Jett had probably been on a thousand dates in the past year, Derreck hadn't been forced to know the exact moment it was happening. This was different. He wasn't angry or jealous, per se. Derreck didn't know what he was feeling, but he wanted to fucking leave here and be a part of whatever Jett was doing.

As if his longing conjured Jett, Derreck caught sight of Kirill making his way through the casino with Jett in tow. They were headed Derreck's way. Derreck stood frozen. Jett was wide-eyed. Kirill looked determined. Derreck didn't know if he was about to be in a fight or get fucked, because both things looked equally possible.

"Your office, now," Kirill said as he passed, heading straight for Derreck's office.

Jett shot him a panicked look and Derreck automatically followed, as if Jett held his heart tied on a tether. Damn. Jett looked sexy. Derreck couldn't stop staring at Jett's ass.

Inside Derreck's office, Kirill shut the door and focused on Derreck. He motioned toward an empty chair. "Sit."

Derreck sat. He couldn't explain why his body kept following Kirill's orders. Jett stood twisting his fingers as Kirill moved to stand at Derreck's back.

Kirill's hand slid across Derreck's throat. Derreck let it happen and he didn't know why. Kirill's fingers dug into Derreck's beard. He massaged. Derreck's eyes tried closing in pleasure. It no longer mattered to his overwhelmed brain that Kirill shouldn't be touching him like this.

"Damn, Jett is right. This beard is sexy as fuck." Before Derreck could respond to that unexpected comment, Kirill's fingers tightened around Derreck's throat, forcing his gaze to stay locked on Jett. "Look at the boy and listen. Hear his truth. It's well past the time he should've talked to you about losing you. Be seen, sexy," Kirill tacked on, obviously talking to Jett.

Jett looked between them. He licked his lips, looking nervous. He shifted from foot to foot before finally focusing on Derreck. "It's not your fault we broke up," Jett said, making Derreck's throat swell. He didn't like the pain in Jett's eyes. Jett moved to stand between Derreck's knees. His hands slid across Derreck's shoulders, as if he couldn't stand not touching Derreck. His gaze never wavered from holding Derreck's stare. "Antonio is your best friend.

It was just a kiss. I was a fucked-up mess and needed help. That kiss did not break us. I did."

Forgetting Kirill's presence, Derreck shook his head. "You wouldn't have left me if I hadn't touched Antonio. That much I know."

Kirill sighed. "This is getting us nowhere." He circled Derreck and stood at Jett's side. "Okay. New approach. Tell me about this kiss. Was it open mouthed with lots of tongue or just a peck?"

Derreck did not want to be doing this, but Jett was there, and they were discussing something they needed to talk about. Still, this was too much detail to be discussing with his boss. "No tongue."

Kirill gave him a sharp nod turned Jett's way and kissed him. It was over as fast as it started. Just a quick press of lips against lips before facing off against Derreck again. "There. If all this heartbreak is only about a kiss, you're even."

Jett nodded, as if in total agreement.

Even though Derreck couldn't explain it, he was sucked in. He shook his head. "It was more than that. There wasn't tongue, but it was still... more."

Jett dropped to his haunches between Derreck's knees. He motioned Derreck closer. "Show me."

There was nothing that could have stopped Derreck from kissing Jett in that moment. He might never have the chance again. Derreck leaned forward and pressed his lips to Jett's before opening his mouth over Jett's bottom lip. He sucked before pulling away again.

Jett glanced up at Kirill. "Did you get that?"

Kirill nodded and helped Jett stand. As Derreck looked on, Kirill drew Jett into his arms and dropped his head. He kissed Jett the way Derreck had. Derreck's breath caught. He shouldn't have been turned on by watching them together, but he was.

Kirill pulled away, looking thoughtful as he focused on Derreck. "I have to say. That's a pretty meaningless kiss. That can't be the way you've always kissed Jett. Surely, if you really want someone, that's not how you do it. So I think Jett is right. There's no way that's what caused you two to split."

Derreck moved to his feet. "That's not how I kiss Jett." That was all the warning he gave before stealing Jett from Kirill's arms and claiming his mouth. He didn't hold back. Derreck kissed Jett with all the pent-up longing of the past year. All the lonely nights and pining for Jett, Derreck poured those things into Jett. He needed Jett to feel his love. Derreck had been so busy missing Jett's presence, he had forgotten how hot they were together. His skin was on fire. Derreck's cock strained against his pants, wanting to burst free.

He felt Kirill move, as if he meant to leave them. Something inside him broke. Derreck's arm shot out. He snagged the front of Kirill's shirt and hauled him forward. Derreck shifted positions, catching the barely suppressed hope in Kirill's eyes before he pulled Kirill into their kiss. Jett didn't back down. Derreck had known he wouldn't. He couldn't explain how he knew. The moment just felt right. Mostly, Derreck wasn't thinking. He was... feeling. Everything about the moment was pure lust, but it was also something else. Derreck held the man he loved, but they felt like more with Kirill there. He was like glue, holding together the fragile tendrils of what they once were.

Jett shoved Derreck's face away, pushing him toward Kirill. "Kiss him. I want to watch."

Before Derreck could argue or tell Jett that he had only gotten carried away, Jett went to work on the buttons of Derreck's shirt and Kirill claimed his mouth. He was unprepared for the heat. Jett's hands were everywhere, caressing bare skin as the two halves of Derreck's shirt fell open. Jett's lips closed around Derreck's nipple. Derreck gasped. Kirill stole his chance to bite Derreck's bottom lip. Derreck almost came right then. He had never been more turned on in his life.

A loud knock landed on Derreck's office door. They jumped apart. All three of them were panting as they eyed each other.

Kirill adjusted his t-shirt, trying to hide his erection. "I'll take care of whatever that is."

As Derreck looked on, Kirill slipped out the door, keeping them hidden from sight. Derreck's gaze slid back Jett's way. Jett looked hungry. Derreck was too confused to make a move. "What just happened?"

Jett chuckled at Derreck's horrified question. He sounded winded. "Well, at the very least, I'd say you just made things pretty awkward with your boss." He flashed Derreck a bright smile. "I'm pretty sure you also just discovered you have a kink."

Derreck shook his head. "I don't have kinks. I'm boring. That was something else. I don't know what, but it wasn't me."

"Oh, Bear. That was you. I'd venture to say that was more you than you've ever shown me." He snatched the flowers Derreck had bought him earlier from Derreck's desk. Jett held them to his chest. "Thank you."

Before Derreck could find out if Jett had thanked

him for the gift or the make-out session, Jett was out the door. Derreck was left alone with nothing but his horror. He had no idea what he had just done. As Jett had pointed out, Kirill was his boss. Derreck's cock twitched. He reached down and adjusted himself. Fuck. He couldn't get Jett's or Kirill's image from his mind. He couldn't separate the two to focus on one.

Derreck ruthlessly buttoned his shirt. He was such an idiot. Here he was, trying to convince Jett to take him back, and the very first fucking thing he did was kiss another man. *Kiss him. I want to watch.* Derreck shook his head. What the fuck was happening to his life? Derreck dropped into his chair. Goddamn, he was one confused idiot. Just another day in Derreck land.

FOUR

WITH THE TOP MISSING FROM HIS JEEP, THE wind ruffled Kirill's hair. The dark parking lot made the stars seem brighter, but Kirill still made a mental note to call someone to complain. Jett wasn't safe walking into his apartment alone at night with this lack of security lighting. Hell, Jett hadn't even noticed Kirill following him home and the boy worked in investigation. He needed someone to take care of him. While Kirill felt certain Derreck could handle the job, Derreck wasn't here right now.

Kirill no longer knew who he was stalking. Unfortunately, he was one hundred percent sure he was stalking someone. Or maybe, he was after some elusive dream. The fantasy that got away. No matter the reason, he had started something he couldn't stop. The moment Derreck had stepped into Jett's path at that bar and grill, Kirill hadn't been able to look away. The desperation for more bled from both men. Kirill had never connected more with anything than he had the longing in Derreck's eyes.

Kirill glanced at his watch. Derreck got off in twenty minutes. If he left now, he could grab Derreck and get back within the hour. Hopefully, Jett was ready for them. Kirill had to strike while the iron was hot. The last thing he wanted was for what started at the casino to cool. Derreck and Jett struck him as over-thinkers. This was definitely one of those times that could kill what they had started.

As he headed back toward the casino, Kirill turned off his brain. He couldn't think about the past right now. All Kirill needed to focus on was the way things had gone in Derreck's office. Kirill drew a steadying breath. The hunger on their faces, goddamn.

Kirill spotted Derreck leaving as he pulled into the employee lot. Kirill steered into his path. Derreck's eyebrows rose at the sight of him. His slightly annoyed expression did nothing to hide the hope in his eyes.

"Get in."

The way Derreck did as ordered without question was hot as fuck.

Kirill didn't say anything else until they were halfway to Jett's. "Do you want to talk about what happened?"

"Not really."

A smile touched Kirill's lips. "Good."

"He's likely to slam the door in our faces." Derreck sounded calm, but there was something underlying in his tone.

"No." Kirill quickly glanced Derreck's way as he made the denial. "He's struggling with a new sense of self. Jett loves being controlled, but he's also been shown that's a bad thing. He needs to see a love that doesn't hurt."

Derreck snorted. "You've been on one date with the guy. So, you know all this how?"

For a moment, Kirill couldn't speak. His throat hurt too much. He finally found his voice. "Because it's like looking in a mirror when I look at him. I used to be him."

"Huh," Derreck said, sounding thoughtful. "You've always struck me as confident to the point of cocky. I wouldn't think you need anyone."

"And you've always struck me as hard to the point of unfeeling," Kirill shot back.

Derreck didn't lose his temper, proving he was probably perfect. "I'm not hard or unfeeling. Just unhappy."

Damn. It took a strong person to freely admit that with no sugarcoating. Kirill couldn't let that bravery stand alone. "Yeah, me too." Kirill didn't say anything else until he was parked and could focus on Derreck. "If it matters at all, kissing you didn't come from nowhere."

For a moment, with his head leaned against the back of the seat, Derreck eyed him in silence. When he spoke, his voice came out quiet but strong. "It matters."

Kirill nodded. "Then let's go kick down that wall Jett is probably already trying to build."

A smile exploded across Derreck's face. "Sounds good." Like that, they were headed for Jett's door. It flew open before they could knock. His hair was wet, as if he had just gotten out of the shower.

Jett looked slightly annoyed. "You're not very good at following people." Kirill snorted. Jett wasn't done. "You did get back with Derreck faster than I expected, though." His gaze slid Derreck's way. "I expected him to put up a fight."

"Why?" Derreck sounded calm and steady. Kirill was fascinated by him.

A sexy smirk touched Jett's lips. His eyes swam with laughter. Kirill couldn't stop looking between them. They knew each other. Understood each other. Kirill almost walked away and left them to it. Then, as one, they looked his way. Kirill felt stripped bare. He had been humming with desire for too long now. Kirill nearly panted beneath the combined power of their stares.

"Get inside." Even Kirill heard the growl to his voice. The pair immediately obeyed. Kirill calmly closed the door behind him as he stalked them inside. Derreck worked on the buttons on his shirt. Jett stood still—like waiting for his orders.

Derreck spoke without looking up from his task. "You should both start stripping. I'm impatient."

Kirill lost the battle against himself. His hand went to his stomach. He tried pressing the flutter into submission. Derreck was in his element now. He was in charge. Kirill peeled off his shirt. Derreck and Jett did the same. The ability to function left Kirill. They were complete opposites. Jett was small and tight. He had a lean runner's body that made Kirill's mouth water at the thought of how flexible he must be. Derreck was wide, cut, and thick. He looked carved from stone. His dark skin looked even darker as his massive arms clasped around Jett. His oddly colored amber gaze locked on Kirill as he pulled Jett back against his chest and went to work on Jett's jeans. He boldly held Kirill's stare as he slid Jett's zipper down. Jett visibly fought the urge to squirm as a flush rose on his cheeks. Derreck set Jett's erection free.

"Hurry, Kirill." Jett sounded needy and desperate, shaking Kirill from his trance.

His hands went to his waistband. Kirill's motions slowed. He might never get this chance again. Kirill wanted them to keep him, so he didn't rush. Instead, Kirill made a show of stripping away the remainder of his clothing. He palmed his cock and stroked while Derreck mimicked him with Jett's erection. Jett whimpered.

Derreck nodded towards the couch the instant Kirill was nude. "Sit."

Kirill moved to do as told.

Derreck kissed Jett's neck. They spoke quietly to each other, making Kirill desperate to know the words they exchanged. With a nod, Jett kicked his way out of his jeans and crossed the room. Kirill couldn't look away. His hand automatically went to his dick. Kirill was so turned on, he couldn't think. He needed relief. Jett moved to stand between Kirill's feet. Then he dropped to his knees. A pant escaped Kirill without his permission. He nearly came as he watched Jett lean forward. Jett held his stare until the last second before his lips locked around Kirill's cock. Kirill sucked in a sharp breath, nearly choking himself. He shot a desperate glance toward where Derreck had been. He was gone. Kirill couldn't think straight with his dick hitting the back of Jett's throat. Everything took on a surreal edge. That feeling doubled when Derreck reappeared.

Nude—like a goddamn sexy god, Derreck moved toward them. His entire body was huge and hard. A condom covered his cock. It shimmered with lube. Derreck set one knee next to Kirill on the couch and claimed Kirill's mouth. It was a hungry kiss. It stole Kirill's breath.

Derreck pulled away. He looked so intense that Kirill could barely breathe beneath his stare. "Fuck Jett's throat. He can take it."

The vibration of Jett chuckling at Derreck's claim around his dick had Kirill's hips leaving the couch, seeking more. All Kirill could do was watch as Derreck moved to his knees behind Jett. Jett made room for him. Kirill couldn't tear his eyes away from the sight of Derreck playing with Jett's ass, stretching him. Derreck positioned his cock against Jett's asshole. His chin lifted. Their gazes collided over

Jett's willing body. Derreck thrust forward in one powerful strike, lifting Jett from the floor with the impact of being impaled. Jett moaned around Kirill's erection.

Kirill's eyes fell shut. "Jesus."

At his breathless curse, Derreck changed angles and thrust again. Jett went from giving a competent blowjob to a passionate bombshell. He yanked Kirill's hips forward, forcing his knees wider and his ass to the edge of the couch. Jett fisted Kirill's cock, tugging while he licked and sucked Kirill's balls. Before Kirill could adjust to the change, Jett was eating his ass. Kirill lost track of everything but the explosion of feelings. He was fairly certain Derreck held his foot, leaving him nowhere to go as Jett licked, sucked, and fingered. Kirill's mind was a mess. Both men were so goddamn beautiful that Kirill wanted to watch them together, but he couldn't even keep track of what happened with his body. All he knew was pleasure. Pressure built and climbed. Jett did some crazy two-fingered shaking of Kirill's cock at the same time as he punched his fingers against that internal button that got him so hot. Kirill exploded. His entire body jackknifed from the couch. He swore he saw stars as his body jerked out of his control. With his face pressed against Kirill's thigh, Jett's open mouth cried out over and over as Derreck pounded inside him. The muscles in Derreck's neck strained as he threw his head back and roared. Kirill couldn't look away. His body shook with aftershocks as the vision of Jett and Derreck in the throes of passion seared into Kirill's brain. Dear god, he had missed this. They couldn't and wouldn't ever know how much he fucking died a little more every day without the pair of men who had left him behind a year ago. Maybe Kirill only used Derreck and Jett as substitutes. He couldn't know. But he did know the pieces of his broken heart cried out for more as he watched himself making all the same mistakes again. Kirill couldn't stop. He needed this.

A SLICE OF SUNSHINE SLAPPED JETT IN THE EYES. He blinked against it as last night's memories slowly intruded. There was a heavy and warm weight across his chest. Jett dropped his chin. A familiar dark and beefy arm rested across Jett's body. He had to take a breath at the instant impact of Derreck's presence in his bed. No one understood how much Jett had missed him. For a moment, Jett feared for his heart if he stayed put.

Jett slipped from the bed. No one else budged. For a moment, Jett stood at the edge of the mattress and stared at the men filling his bed. He felt strangely calm. Like a deep-seated peace had settled in his gut, Jett felt full.

He scooped Derreck's shirt from the floor and slipped his arms inside. Since Derreck was like three of Jett put together, the button-down shirt fell past Jett's knees. He disappeared inside the material, overwhelmed by the scent of Derreck's cologne. Jett's eyes fell closed. He fought the urge to bury his face in the material and inhale. His gaze slid back to the men. Butterflies stirred in his stomach. He had been terrified of backsliding. Jett didn't want to give in to temptation and end up weak again. While wearing Derreck's shirt and staring at the two men he had pleasured, Jett felt like he could take over the world. He wasn't dependent upon them for happiness. It was the morning after, and he wasn't less for having been with them.

Since Jett honestly didn't know how to feel, he did his usual thing. Ran to the bathroom. Made coffee. Jett tiptoed around his house and tried not to think too hard. It wasn't until he stood still in the silence of his kitchen that Jett's brain went into overdrive. He couldn't step back from this. Jett had known opening the door to Derreck meant more than letting the man into his apartment; he had let Derreck back in his mind and heart. Kirill... that was another matter. Another flutter of something stirred in Jett's stomach. There was something a bit dark about Kirill. He was secretive. Kirill joined them for some reason all his own and Jett wanted to know what he kept hidden. Jett suppressed a chuckle. He truly had jumped back into sex with both feet. Two men. Wow. It didn't seem likely he could keep them both.

Movement outside the kitchen caught Jett's eye. He leaned back against the counter. With a cup of coffee held between his hands, warming them, Jett watched Kirill quietly search for his clothes—like a man bent on escaping without notice.

"Are you sneaking away?"

Kirill's gaze shot to where Jett stood inside the darkened kitchen. A sexy smile touched his lips. He closed the distance between them and crowded Jett's space. "No. I have to get showered and get to work. Derreck still has a few hours before he's scheduled to be there. I was trying not to wake him."

Jett side-eyed him. "Are you sure? It looked like sneaking to me."

Kirill chuckled. "I thought you had already run out on us."

"It's my apartment." Jett's cheeks ached from smiling.

Kirill stole the coffee from Jett's hand, drank, and then set it aside. With nothing left to block him, Kirill shuffled closer. He dipped his chin and touched his lips to Jett's. It was only a sweet brushing of lips against lips. "I'm very happy to have met you," Kirill said as he moved to skim his lips across Jett's cheek. He kept going until he lightly kissed the shell of Jett's ear. "Does this count as our third or fourth date?"

Jett swept his hands up Kirill's bare chest. He couldn't keep his eyes open with Kirill's lips on his skin. "I don't know anymore."

"Maybe I should stop counting then." His tongue traced the shape of Jett's ear. Jett's body was on fire. "Have a good day, baby." Jett nearly melted to the floor as Kirill pulled away. He fought the urge to beg Kirill to stay as he watched Kirill dress. With a final scorching glance Jett's way, Kirill let himself out.

For a long moment, Jett stood in the silence, listening to nothing but the tick of the clock on the wall. Images flashed through his mind. Kirill staring at him with flushed cheeks and hooded eyes.

Derreck's fingers making indentions on Jett's skin as he held Jett in place. Jett gasped out a breath. It sounded loud in the otherwise silent kitchen. The hunger won. Jett's feet moved without his permission until he stood, hovering over Derreck's sleeping form.

With one arm slung across his eyes and the sheet barely covering the lower half of his body, Derreck's massive chest was a bare feast for Jett's eyes. He wanted more. Jett snagged the corner of the sheet and slowly dragged it lower. His mouth watered as Derreck's cock came into view. Even soft, he was huge. Jett had almost forgotten what it was like to be filled to overflowing with Derreck's dick. He was so goddamn delicious.

Jett set one knee on the bed, being careful not to wake Derreck. Moving slow, he crawled onto the mattress before tossing one leg over Derreck, straddling his body. Derreck stirred as Jett settled on Derreck's chest. As he pressed his ear against Derreck's heartbeat, Derreck's arms encircled him. Jett smiled as Derreck grabbed a handful of comforter and pulled the blankets over them. His eyes fell closed as he listened to the steady thump against his ear.

"I love you."

Jett swallowed at the grumble that sounded even deeper with his ear pressed to Derreck's chest. His eyes burned. He missed being held and hearing those words. Derreck had always said them when he thought Jett wouldn't hear. This was different and Jett was braver now.

He kissed Derreck's chest. "I love you too."

Derreck's arms tightened around him. Jett drew a slow breath. This was where he was meant to be. He couldn't lose sight of that again. They would be better. Derreck would see. Jett would fix them.

FIVE

No matter how hard he tried, Derreck couldn't stop being on the lookout for Kirill. He had sneaked away before Derreck could say goodbye or... hell, he didn't know. Things were weird now. The more Derreck thought about it, the more he realized how true Kirill's claim was—their kiss hadn't started from nothing. Over the past year of working together, they had butted heads many times. Looking back on things, Derreck saw their heated exchanges leaned heavier on the heat side of things than he had wanted to admit. Mostly, he had ignored his feelings because he had never stopped loving Jett. There had always been a part of Derreck that had known his time with Jett wasn't over. Derreck had been in a state of holding, waiting until he had Jett back in his arms. That knowledge hadn't stopped Derreck from —on some visceral level—gravitating toward Kirill. Now he needed to see if Kirill looked at him any differently or if this powerful thing happening between the three of them was all in Derreck's head.

Derreck spotted Kirill weaving his way through the gaming floor. He had the sleeves of his pink dress shirt rolled up to his elbows, showing off his sexy forearms. His tan dress pants clung to his round ass. Derreck couldn't look away. With his head down, eyeing the paperwork in his hand, Kirill's dark hair fell across one eye. Derreck's palms itched to push it aside, tucking it behind his ear. Kirill's gaze lifted and skimmed the room, skirting right over Derreck like he wasn't there. The breath left Derreck's lungs in a whoosh. He tried not to panic. They were at work. Kirill and he held management positions. They couldn't be who they were last night while here. Derreck ignored the tiny voice in the back of his mind, reminding him they had kissed here too last night.

With his heart in his throat, Derreck got back to work. He had a ton of paperwork in his office, needing his attention. Not to mention, he had a few tables to check. Fuck. Derreck couldn't think straight. He smiled at everyone he passed, even though he didn't feel it. Derreck fought the urge to rush to his office and text Jett, confessing his fears. The thought of Jett brought with it another wave of worries. What if Kirill hadn't been interested in Derreck at all? It was possible, after one date with Jett, Kirill had seen there was only one way to have Jett—through Derreck. Goddamn. He couldn't breathe. Derreck needed to get inside his office before he had a full-blown panic attack. Maybe Kirill planned to steal Jett away and Derreck would be left alone in the world again. He could feel the walls closing in on him.

Derreck got one foot inside his office when he found himself hauled the rest of the way inside. The door slammed closed behind him. Kirill overcame him. His hands were everywhere as he kissed Derreck deep. His tongue stroked, seeking more, and stealing Derreck's breath. Derreck buried his fingers in Kirill's hair and hung on. He had gone a year without feeling anything. In just a couple of days, Derreck had gone from nothing to everything.

By the time Kirill pulled away, he tightly held Derreck's shirt and gasped for air. He stared at Derreck's lips. "I should let you work."

A chuckle rose and stuck in Derreck's throat.

Happiness owned him in every way. "Probably, since you're my boss, but I'm not complaining."

Kirill's gaze lifted. He looked every bit as consumed as Derreck felt. "I'm trying not to embarrass you. As you said, I'm your boss. You have to work with everyone here."

Derreck shrugged. "Pretty much everyone here was here when Antonio owned the place. They're all accustomed to me being more than the usual employee, but I get it. You have people to answer to as well." Derreck couldn't miss his chance to say something to Kirill he had always wanted to say. "I can't even imagine being the one who has to directly answer to a mafia boss." After all, everyone knew the Russian mafia owned Luna. No one talked about it, but Vegas was Kapra territory. Even though Zander Kapra lived in California, he owned everything and everyone in this town and on the west coast, whether they realized it or not.

One corner of Kirill's mouth lifted. He took a step back. He didn't quite meet Derreck's stare. "I wouldn't want to work for anyone else." His gaze finally locked on Derreck. The power of having his attention was immense. Derreck couldn't look anywhere else. "Let Jett know I have plans for you two tonight."

"Should I feel weird about this?" Derreck said, giving voice to the one thought he had been avoiding looking too closely at since last night.

A rumble of laughter vibrated from Kirill. "I know it's hard not to overthink things, especially since I understand how much you love Jett, but just don't. Okay?" Kirill visibly swallowed, making it impossible for Derreck to respond. There was something in Kirill's eyes. "Give me a little time before you shut me out."

A sardonic smile pulled at Derreck's lips. "Give me a little time before you expect the worst from me."

Kirill's gaze sharpened. "I think you're amazing. Always have." With that bombshell hanging between them, Kirill hurried away, leaving Derreck alone with nothing but a hard-on and his thoughts.

Derreck dug out his phone and called Jett. A smile stretched his lips when Jett answered on the first ring.

"Your number is the same. You didn't respond to my text the other night."

Derreck moved to sit at his desk. "Hello, sweet angel. Yes. My number hasn't changed. I'm sorry I didn't respond to your text the other night. When it came in, I was driving. By the time I got home, I had convinced myself that you didn't really want to hear from me again."

"Oh. Okay."

Damn. Derreck didn't know how someone could love someone as much as Derreck loved Jett and not explode. "What are you doing right now?"

"Following this guy through the grocery store, waiting to catch him lifting something heavy. You know, the usual."

An unwanted hint of irritation rose inside Derreck. "Isn't that dangerous?"

"Not really." Jett sounded oddly disappointed.

Derreck didn't feel better. "But what if he spots you following him?"

A sexy chuckle vibrated through the phone and caressed his ear. "I've been getting my ass kicked my whole life, Bear. At least now I'm getting paid. Plus, I'm not worried. For once in my life, I'm actually pretty good at something. I'm good at this."

The pride in Jett's voice made it impossible for Derreck to keep arguing. He decided to change the subject. "Kirill wanted me to let you know he has plans for us tonight." Derreck held his breath. They hadn't exactly talked about anything. For all Derreck knew, Jett wouldn't see them again.

"Interesting. What does he have planned?"

Derreck released his pent breath. "I don't know. It's a surprise, I'm guessing."

Jett made a humming sound that had Derreck wishing he could feel it around his cock. "No one wants to go first, so I will. What are we doing here? The three of us, I mean." Jett's question was like cold water thrown in Derreck's face. He didn't want to say the wrong thing and lose Jett again.

"I hope we're building something." Derreck's tie felt too tight. He loosened it as he tried explaining his thoughts. "From the first time I saw you, I was instantly enthralled. I thought you were like this wild beauty I could never have or handle. Plus, you were dating Antonio, so I felt all sorts of wrong for wanting you so badly." A smile tugged at Derreck's lips as the memories washed over him. "Then, bit by bit, you felt less wrong all the time. I think... never mind." Derreck hated himself for being weak, but he didn't want to lose Jett again.

"Finish your thoughts." Jett sounded breathless— like he needed to know.

Derreck took a breath. "I think maybe one of the reasons I was so scared to lose Antonio is because having you two together had always been such a huge fantasy for me. Losing him permanently to Bay meant giving up any chance of watching you the way I watched you last night."

For a moment, silence met his confession. Finally, Jett cleared his throat. "What about Kirill? Is he just convenient?"

A snort escaped Derreck without thought. "There's nothing convenient about Kirill. He's my boss and I'm not sure he's ever even particularly liked me, but... goddamn. I don't know, angel. Something happened between the three of us last night and I can't believe for one second I'm the only one who felt it. I didn't plan this, nor do I think this is a great idea. But I'm in love with you. Always have been. And I think Kirill completes us in some way I can't explain. I think we need him, and I think he needs us."

To Derreck's surprise, Jett didn't balk. "I agree. You know, I should psychoanalyze you and say that you need this type of relationship because you never had a family, and the whole throuple relationship dynamic makes you feel a little more whole. I won't do that, though."

Derreck couldn't stop smiling. "I'm glad you spared me the psychoanalysis. You said twice in the same sentence that this is a relationship, so I won't point out that you need this relationship too for almost the same reason."

"Oh, there's no need to psychoanalyze me, Bear. I've had enough therapy to know myself." Derreck heard a car door close. Jett's voice turned sultry, as if they were alone now. "Plus, I'm not ashamed to admit that I like to watch and be watched. Not to mention, I'm in love with you. I can't begin to tell you how it felt having you inside me and knowing you watched me suck Kirill's dick. No one on the planet has ever set me free and made me feel as powerful as you do." Jett took an audible breath. The hair stood on the back of Derreck's neck. He swore he felt the power of Jett's next words before they were spoken. "If we're doing this, then this is it. Kirill and I have to be enough for you. I can't get my heart broken by you again, Bear. I just can't."

Derreck rubbed his chest. While he had known he had hurt Jett, Jett had been so strong these last few days that Derreck hadn't been forced to truly face his misdeeds. He was facing them now. It was ugly inside Derreck's head. He swallowed down his pain to focus on Jett's. "I know leaving me was one of the best things you've ever done for yourself. You're stronger now. But you will never understand how much hurting you completely gutted me. I believe you when you say that kiss didn't break us, but it broke me. For as long as I live, I'll never forgive myself. I can't live through that again either. I just can't."

"Then I guess we'll have to make us work this time." The way Jett said those words, so calm and sure, he set Derreck at ease. Everything would be okay. Things were different, but different was good. They would be fine. Kirill had them now. Derreck didn't know how he knew Kirill would make them whole. He just knew.

THE LAST THING KIRILL WANTED WAS TO LET HIS heart get drawn into things. It was obvious Derreck and Jett were working out their relationship kinks. Kirill would end up the loser in that scenario every single time. All the foresight in the world didn't make Kirill's body burn any less. When he had walked past Derreck without meeting his gaze earlier, something inside Kirill had cried out. He hadn't been able to stop himself from making it right. Now his mind was whirling with ideas of making the impossible possible. A tiny voice—traitorous to his heart—teased Kirill. It said Kirill could win them. So he did something he didn't do anywhere near often enough. He hid in his office and called Zander.

"Hello?"

Kirill smiled at the sound of Zander's voice. He pictured the man's perfect features drawn tight with annoyance. "Did I catch you at a bad time?"

"Not at all." Zander's voice lost its harsh edge. "The caller ID showed the Vegas Luna and I expected another whiney complaint about something below my pay grade. I'm happy to hear it is you. It's been a few months."

Kirill winced at the subtle admonishment. "Yes. Sorry, cousin. Staying on top of things here keeps me busy, but I've missed your voice." Even Kirill heard the way his Russian accent deepened while hearing it mimicked.

"You do realize you're allowed to delegate and enjoy life, do you not?"

A chuckle rose in Kirill's throat. Even though he had looked up to Zander as a small child, he hadn't always been a part of Zander's life. In fact, Kirill had thought Zander dead until a few years back when Zander brought him here to live in the States. Sometimes, the truth was worse. "I would never want you to think you made the wrong decision by putting me in this position."

Zander snorted. "Don't be ridiculous."

Kirill couldn't stop smiling. Sometimes, Kirill was torn right down the middle. Zander had given him an amazing and lucrative position in Vegas, but Zander was in California. Kirill didn't have anyone here. "How is that sexy husband of yours?"

"He's good. I'll tell him you asked."

"And everyone else?"

"Everyone here is good. What's going on?" Zander asked, showing his usual level of astuteness. "You sound as if you have nothing to say and are simply stalling for discomfort purposes."

Kirill shook his head. There was no one else in the world like Zander. "I'd like to come home tonight."

Zander didn't miss a beat. "That's fine. Call the pilot and give him a time. He'll be there."

"I'd like to bring a couple of people with me." Kirill held his breath. Silence met his words.

Finally, Zander broke. "Tell me."

Kirill leaned back in his chair and stared at the ceiling. "Oh, you know me. I'm making all the same mistakes I always do."

"Is it the same mistakes or similar mistakes with different people?"

A chuckle slipped from Kirill. "The second one."

"That is fine, then. You are not dead, Kirill. Your heart knows what it wants. It is no mistake to keep trying. Giving up is the only failure."

"Hmmm," Kirill hummed, unsure if he believed. "To be honest, I have no idea what I'm doing. I'm like a stray dog, hoping someone will take me in."

A loud snort sounded through the phone. "For that to be true, you'd have to take advantage of others. If anything, you're the one who can't stop taking in strays until they turn on you. But you haven't let that stop you from trying to save people. That's what makes you better than everyone else."

Kirill smiled. Zander was a good person. "Talking to you is always good for my ego."

"I should let you go, then," Zander said with a laugh. "Your ego needs no stroking."

That was true. Despite his maudlin thoughts, Kirill knew what he brought to the table. "You just wish to rush me from the phone so you can molest your husband."

"Possibly."

Laughter gathered in Kirill's throat. He swallowed it. "Okay. I'll let you get to it, then. Maybe I'll see you while I'm in town this weekend."

"I won't hold my breath."

Kirill rolled his eyes at Zander's words, even

though Zander was right. He doubted he would come up for air once he had Jett and Derreck to himself. "Talk soon."

"Agreed," Zander said, disconnecting their call.

Kirill set the phone back in its cradle and started making plans. He wouldn't think too much from this point on. Kirill wanted Derreck and Jett. That was all. He would enjoy them until they were done. Not every adventure was permanent. This was no different... or perhaps it was. Kirill no longer knew how to tell.

SIX

ALL DAY, JETT HAD FORCED HIMSELF TO WORK
while keeping his mind blank. Everything he had
sworn he wouldn't do again, Jett had already jumped
back into with both feet. He honestly thought he had
turned the page on his old life. The first hint of
affection someone gave him, Jett begged for more. He
needed to stop. Take a breath. Get his priorities back
in order. Derreck had sworn he wouldn't hurt Jett.
Jett wasn't worried about that. Derreck wasn't the
problem. Jett was. He was the one who always ended
up destroying himself. Dating Kirill and Derreck
meant potentially destroying two people along with
himself. Derreck had misunderstood earlier when
Jett had said he couldn't go through what he had

before. Derreck being Derreck, he had immediately put the blame on himself. It didn't seem to matter how many times or ways Jett explained that he had been the one who needed help. Jett couldn't let the dark voices in again. He just couldn't. Jett wouldn't live like that again.

A knock made Jett jump. His gaze shot to the clock. He had been so wrapped up in his thoughts, he had forgotten Kirill had plans for them tonight. Jett crossed the room and opened the door. He bit back a smile at the sight greeting him.

"Is this the new way of things?" Jett asked the moment he set eyes on his gorgeous men. Kirill and Derreck stood side by side on his stoop, just as they had last night. They wore matching smiles. Jett shook his head. "How am I supposed to stand against you two? Are you two coming in or am I coming out?"

Derreck looked Kirill's way, proving he didn't know any more than Jett did about their plans. "Don't ask me," Derreck said, answering Jett without looking away from Kirill. "I asked if I'd ever be allowed to change out of my work clothes again and my question went unanswered."

Kirill smirked. "You're supposed to enjoy a

surprise." He tossed a heated glance Derreck's way. His wickedness doubled. "Besides, I stopped by your place and let you change and pack a bag." Jett wondered what else happened while they were at Derreck's place. Before he could ask, Kirill focused on Jett. "It's your turn now. Grab an overnight bag, angel. We have a flight to catch."

The claim took Jett by surprise. "A flight? I have to work Monday."

Kirill shrugged. "We all do."

Jett bit back a sigh. He had already lost all control. He waved them inside. "It'll take me a minute to get my stuff together." He closed the door behind the pair. "Do I get any hints about the type of weather I should be packing for or anything?" Jett turned back toward the pair and found himself overcome. It happened so fast, Jett didn't know who initiated the kiss. All he knew was heat and tongues. He didn't know which way to turn as first one tongue and then another stroked his. There were hands everywhere. He couldn't breathe or think.

"Why aren't you packed yet?" Kirill asked as he moved to kiss Jett's neck.

"Yeah. We're waiting," Derreck chimed in, dragging a laugh from Jett.

"Ugh. You two. It's not fair to always gang up on me."

Kirill hummed. "Mhmm, gang."

Derreck mimicked Kirill's hum against Jett's lips. "Up."

With a snort, Jett found the strength to push them away and head for the bedroom. He pressed his hands to his cheeks. Jett couldn't stop smiling. He couldn't recall ever being this happy. It was just so damn ridiculous. People didn't happily date two people at the same time, right? This was crazy. Surely, this whole thing would explode in their faces. Jett glanced over his shoulder. Kirill and Derreck watched him go with matching hungry stares. He nearly missed a step. All through packing two days' worth of clothes, Jett floated in a haze while questions bombarded him. At least one of them should be jealous. Shouldn't they? When Jett thought about Derreck kissing Antonio, he wanted to storm back into the living room and punch Derreck in the balls. Yet Jett knew Derreck had been alone with Kirill today. At the very least, they had kissed without him there. He searched his heart. All he felt was envious. He wished he had been there to enjoy it. It was all so damn strange. It was like he was embracing some part of himself he hadn't realized he neglected. Or maybe he just liked them both so much, he wasn't willing to give up either man. Jett wanted to ride this out until its inevitable messy end.

"Are you okay?"

At Kirill's sudden appearance, Jett realized he had been standing over his packed bag and staring at nothing for god only knew how long. Jett picked up his bag. "Yeah. Sorry. I guess I got lost in my thoughts."

Kirill moved closer. "Were at least one of those thoughts about me?"

He looked so sexy in his black t-shirt and dark jeans. His light blue eyes looked even lighter with his dark hair hanging in his eyes. He was a bit of a bad boy. Jett could feel it in his bones. "I don't know if I should admit to thinking about you. You strike me as the type to take advantage."

"I take that as a yes, and yes I plan to take advantage." With that warning hanging between them, Kirill hauled Jett forward and kissed him. A wave of neediness washed over Jett. He wanted to be held and kissed. Petted. Loved. As if Kirill read his mind, he kissed Jett sweetly. Softly. Jett's heart beat a little faster. He'd never expected this one. Maybe a small part of him had believed Derreck would show back up one day, but he hadn't seen Kirill coming.

"I'm beginning to think you want me more than just a little."

Kirill's quiet assessment surprised a laugh from Jett. "What gave me away? Did I hold your stare a little too long? Or maybe when I licked your cock, I wore just a certain expression."

Kirill didn't laugh as Jett hoped. Instead, Kirill's gaze moved over Jett's face, as if searching for something only he could see. "No," he said finally. "Anyone can blow someone, even if they hate them. You keep letting me see the real you. I don't think you do that very often or with many people."

Fuck. He was right. Jett normally hid behind a mask. He was a pretender, showing people what they wanted to see. The more time Jett spent with Kirill, the less he hid. Jett needed to be careful. Otherwise, he might find himself in love with two men. Then what would he do? Surely he would be forced to choose. What had he started?

WHEN KIRILL SAID THEY HAD A PLANE TO CATCH,

Derreck hadn't expected Kirill meant a private plane. Since Derreck had driven Antonio several times to the private airstrip, he had known exactly where Kirill was headed halfway to the airport. Still, he hadn't said a word. Even when Jett tossed him a questioning look on the sly, Derreck had simply shaken his head as they climbed the steps into a private jet.

Jett obviously decided to give up on Derreck when Derreck wouldn't commiserate with him. Instead, he went after Kirill. "Um, what's going on? This plane has a bedroom."

"So it does," Kirill said with a chuckle, doing nothing to squelch their curiosity.

While Kirill spoke with the pilot, Derreck and Jett sat on a couch that lined one side of the plane. Derreck leaned Jett's way. "I think the general manager position pays a lot more than what I'm making at Luna."

Jett covered a snort.

Kirill glanced their way and winked. Derreck knew Kirill was too far away to have heard his comment. That meant he simply couldn't stop himself from looking at them. Derreck linked fingers with Jett. His heart beat a little faster with Jett's hand in his and his gaze locked on Kirill. He didn't know where they were headed—literally or figuratively—but he was along for the whole ride.

Derreck didn't have to wait long to learn their destination. Not only did time pass in the blink of an eye with Kirill talking nonstop about growing up in Russia, they weren't in the air that long. Less than two hours later, they were met by a private car in a new town.

Jett practically danced on the way to the car. "I smell the ocean. Where are we?"

A bright smile lit Kirill's face at Jett's enthusiasm. "San Diego."

"Really? I've only been here once, and I drove. Also, it was a long time ago. Right after I got my license." Jett chuckled. He didn't look their way as he spoke. "I had to wait until I was seventeen, because my dad wouldn't let me drive. I ran away and had this big plan to come to California, and I don't know what I thought would happen here, but it didn't. I just ended up back in Vegas and living with an asshole of a different breed. But those few days here were the first taste of freedom I had after years of abuse. It's no wonder I remember the smell, I guess."

Kirill glanced at Derreck with his eyebrows raised in question. Derreck gave him a short nod, letting him know the abuse was every bit as bad as Kirill feared—no matter how light Jett kept his tone.

Kirill's chest expanded with a deep breath and an obviously faked smile touched his lips. "I imagine you took this town by storm."

Jett snorted as he slid inside the car. "Okay." The sarcasm in Jett's voice couldn't be missed.

Kirill didn't press for more.

Derreck didn't want to know. He imagined Jett had a million horror stories he never shared. Derreck hated himself every time he thought about that, because he was one of those stories. Rather than digging for info on their destination, Derreck chose to make the ride in silence. There was a pressure sitting on his chest. His gaze kept sliding Jett's way. A small part of him wished he hadn't pursued Jett. Being with Jett had been the first step toward losing his oldest friend. Maybe Antonio still spoke to Derreck, but they weren't the same as they had once been. That downhill spiral had led to Derreck also losing Jett. Now things felt different. It was still love, and those emotions still owned him, but Derreck wasn't confident that Jett would stick around. Jett was too young. Too beautiful. Inside, Derreck would always be the homeless guy Antonio rescued. He couldn't imagine anyone keeping him.

Derreck's gaze slid Kirill's way. Kirill stared back. For a moment, Derreck swore Kirill could read his mind. He looked intense—almost angry. This was the man for Jett. Kirill would never let anything bad happen to Jett. He was exactly the person Jett needed. Kirill would hold the three of them together. Derreck felt that in his gut. Possessiveness roared to life in Derreck's chest. He wanted this new dynamic with something akin to desperation. Derreck would do whatever it took.

Kirill turned his head, breaking the spell as they turned down a driveway leading to a gorgeous house. It wasn't massive like an estate, but it was pretty damn big. It was too dark to tell the exact color, but Derreck imagined it was white by the way it stood out in the dark.

"Welcome home, Mr. Kapra," the driver said as he killed the engine in front of the house.

Derreck's breath left him in a whoosh. Since the moment Kirill had been introduced to the staff, he had insisted on being called Kirill or Mr. Kirill. It hadn't once occurred to Derreck that Kirill might have the general manager position at such a young age because he was related to the owner of Luna. He was related to the mafia. Derreck's mind was blown.

He didn't know how to react or what to say, so he held his tongue.

Jett had no such qualms. "Oh my god. This is your house? You have a house in California." Jett looked and sounded as blown away as Derreck felt, but not for the same reasons. "Jesus Christ. This place is nice," Jett said as he fought the driver for his bags.

Kirill glanced around as if seeing the place for the first time. "Yeah. I haven't convinced myself to sell the place yet. When Zander offered me the general manager position in Vegas last year, we discussed it being a temporary move. He left it up to me. If I love the job, it's mine and I'll stay in Vegas. If I want to come home, I can. So I haven't sold yet."

"Zander, as in Zander Kapra? The guy who owns Luna? Wait. Your last name is Kapra too?"

At Jett's questions, Kirill nodded. "We're cousins."

"Wow." Jett looked impressed.

Derreck heard something else beneath Kirill's voice. He missed this place. "So you still haven't decided to stay in Vegas."

At Derreck's observation, Jett's expression turned sad—like he too realized Kirill didn't see them as permanent, but a smile exploded across Kirill's face. "I'm glad I never sold. Otherwise, I would've missed this moment. I like seeing both of you this surprised," he said as they dragged the bags through the door and the lights inside flared to life. "What do you two want to do first?"

Jett dropped his bags and bounced from place to place, looking in rooms and out windows. He practically danced in place in his excitement. "I want to swim."

Derreck groaned. "Why is everyone always trying to drag me out into the sun? Black people burn too, you know?"

Jett flashed him a sweet smile that held a hint of naughtiness. "First off, it's currently nighttime. But even if it wasn't, that's what sunscreen is for, Bear, and I'm right here, ready to rub you down with any product you need."

Damn. Derreck couldn't argue with that, but he still found a way. "I didn't pack swim trunks, since I didn't know where we were going."

A soft and wicked-sounding chuckle fell from Kirill's lips. "You won't need those here. No one can see you but us."

A growl rose in Derreck's throat. He swallowed the sound. It didn't look like he would get out of this. He took a breath. "Fine." He motioned toward the

French doors where the lit pool glimmered on the other side. "Let's go."

Jett squealed.

Derreck shook his head. He didn't really like swimming pools or any body of water for that matter, but Jett's excitement was too much to ignore.

Jett headed for the door and peeked his head outside. "*Ooooh*, there's a hot tub too."

Okay. He kind of liked that. Derreck crossed the room. As he passed Kirill, his hand automatically went to Kirill's stomach. He stroked. Their gazes met and held for a moment. Derreck's breath caught at the heat in Kirill's eyes, but he didn't budge. Instead, Kirill let Derreck pass.

Derreck glanced behind him as he realized Kirill wasn't joining them. "Aren't you coming?"

Kirill shook his head. "I'll take everyone's bags to my bedroom and grab some towels. You two go ahead."

Jett was already outside stripping. That had Derreck giving Kirill his space and stepping outside. While Derreck watched, Jett wasted no time. He stripped and jumped into the pool. Jett came up gasping.

"Holy shit. It's cold. I wasn't expecting that."

With a laugh, Derreck scooped up Jett's clothes

and carried them to the closest lounge chair. He kicked off his shoes and peeled off his shirt. Jett swam to the edge of the pool and openly watched. Derreck held his stare and finished undressing. He loved the way Jett looked at him—like he hung the moon. No one else had ever looked at Derreck like Jett did.

Once he was nude, Derreck headed for the smaller steaming pool. "I'll be over here," he said as he sank into the hot tub. While he adjusted the jets and got the water churning, Jett climbed from the pool. Derreck chuckled at the sight of Jett running from the pool to the hot tub.

"Goddamn. I'm really cold now."

Derreck opened his arms as Jett climbed in beside him. "Come to Papa. I'll keep you warm."

"Mhmm. I do like the sound of that," Jett said as he settled in with Derreck's arm draped over his shoulders. His palm slid up Derreck's bare thigh. The back door opened, and Kirill stepped out with towels in hand. His gaze swept the backyard before landing on them. He headed their way and dropped the towels on the lounge chair with the clothes before coming to stand over them.

"You two look cozy."

Jett flashed a bright smile. "The pool was cold."

"Shit." Kirill glanced around. "I didn't think about that. I should turn the heat up."

Jett waved off his words. "Don't worry about it. I'm happy here. Are you coming in?"

Instead of answering, Kirill dropped to the ground and sat beside them. "You look happy. I want to stare at you all night."

Jett's hand moved higher up Derreck's thigh. Derreck couldn't focus on anything else. Thankfully, Jett took control of the conversation. "I'm super confused by you."

Kirill cocked his head to one side. "How so?"

Jett motioned wildly with his free hand. "This place. You have this gorgeous house and access to a private plane. Yet you're choosing to live in a hotel in Vegas. You're a complete mystery to me."

Kirill shook his head. "There's no secret to uncover here. I had a life here. Now I have a life in Vegas."

"But you haven't chosen between the two," Jett said, pushing while pointing out the obvious.

"Maybe I'm waiting for the right life to choose me," Kirill said as he came to his feet. He stripped off his shirt and tossed it aside. "But I think you're missing the big picture."

Derreck's gaze dropped to Kirill's hands as he

reached for the button on his jeans. With Jett's hand inches from his cock and Kirill doing a striptease, Derreck wasn't paying much attention to the conversation.

Jett held up his end. "What's the big picture?"

Kirill finished undressing and joined them in the hot tub, sandwiching Jett between Derreck and him before responding. "I brought you two here, showing you more of my life than anyone else has seen in a long time. You can't claim to not know me after this weekend." He turned a heated stare their way. "You two can't claim you don't know I want you in more than just my bed. Whichever life I choose, I want you both with me."

Kirill officially had Derreck's full attention. Someone had to be the first to say it, and Kirill had. This wasn't about sex.

Jett gave a sharp nod, as if his mind was set. "Me too. I want to do this."

They looked Derreck's way. Derreck felt a wicked smile pull at his lips. They were both beautiful and waiting for him. "I want this." It was like a giant boulder lifted from Derreck's chest, allowing him to breathe. They were in this together. No game playing or jealousy. It was fucking amazing.

FOR HALF A SECOND, KIRILL HAD TRULY believed he could sit beside the hot tub and play the voyeur. The way Derreck kept eyeing them both while Jett tried to carry on a conversation was too much. Kirill had to join them. He imagined Derreck's patience would snap any second and he wanted to be a part of that. Kirill decided to push him over the edge. He kissed Jett's ear. Derreck made a sound—like his cock had been caressed.

Kirill touched Jett's chin and urged him to meet Kirill's stare. "I want to fuck you." Jett released a stuttered gasp as Kirill's gaze slid Derreck's way, and he added, "While he fucks me."

"Jesus." The breathless curse made Derreck sound horny as hell. That was exactly how Kirill wanted him.

"You should let me take you to bed," Kirill said, looking between the pair.

Derreck stood, as if impatience brought him to his feet. Kirill bit back a smile as he stood and helped Jett up. Together, they grabbed the towels and headed inside. Kirill let his hunger grow as heated looks passed between them. Inside, Kirill led the way to his bedroom. It was almost like there was a calm acceptance between them. They wanted one another. The hunger and desperation were real, but they each knew something bigger than lust—they had time. This wasn't a weekend fling where they needed to fuck as much and as often as possible because they would never get another chance. They were building something new and strong. Stunning.

Kirill moved to the bathroom inside his bedroom, found a bottle of lube and some condoms, and returned. Jett eyed Kirill's tall bed before scrambling up. A chuckle escaped Kirill at the sight. It quickly died away as Jett settled onto his back and openly stroked his dick. Kirill's gaze slid Derreck's way. He was nude and huge. Everything about him screamed patience except the desperation in his eyes.

"Get on the bed," Derreck demanded. "Let me watch you for a moment."

A stuttered breath left Kirill. He climbed onto the mattress and pumped some lube into his hand. Kirill made a show of suiting up and oiling Jett's asshole. Jett squirmed, writhing for more. His sexy dick leaked on his stomach, making Kirill's mouth water. Everything about Jett was pretty. He was small and fragile. Jett made Kirill want to protect him and fuck him. Kirill's mind was a mess. He was torn between his belief that nothing good could come of this and his desire to make them work. Kirill didn't think he had ever wanted anything as much as he wanted this relationship. His thoughts dried up as he parted Jett's perfect ass cheeks. Kirill's stomach muscles cramped as he stared down at Jett's lubed hole.

"Please?"

Kirill's gaze shot to Jett's face. His sweet brown eyes pleaded for Kirill to fuck him. Kirill couldn't wait any longer. He swiped his crown across Jett's asshole. Jett whimpered. Derreck growled. Kirill's eyes fell closed as the combined sounds caressed his ears. He thrust, impaling Jett. Jett cried out. Kirill rocked, finding a rhythm that kept Jett openly panting. The bed shifted as Derreck joined them.

"Goddamn. You two are hot as hell. I can't wait any longer."

Kirill found himself flattened against Jett. He kissed and nipped at Jett's chest as beefy fingers probed and stretched his asshole. Kirill couldn't be still. He squirmed, making Jett whimper. Kirill tongued Jett's nipple, trying to cling to something tangible. It had been a long time since anything other than dildos had been inside his ass and Kirill had never been with anyone as big as Derreck. It was almost terrifying. Then Derreck's crown slipped inside him. Derreck froze, giving him time to adjust. He changed angles and slipped a little farther in. Kirill open mouth gasped for air against Jett's chest. Derreck rocked, massaging that internal button that drove him mad. Something inside Kirill snapped.

Even though he was in the middle, he took control. He thrust inside Jett and then rocked back on Derreck. Kirill didn't try to please. His every thought was on that pattern—giving and taking. It felt too good for him to stop. It was just slippery and sweaty sex. He couldn't get enough. Teeth and tongues seemed to be everywhere. He no longer knew who made what sound. A haze coated reality as Kirill fought to reach the oblivion Jett and Derreck promised. Pressure grew and built, making him work harder. His muscles screamed at the odd angles he attempted to best get what he wanted. Jett cried out and his asshole sucked. Air no longer mattered as Jett's body stole Kirill's soul. A spasm rocked him as ecstasy made him jerk uncontrollably. Derreck held his throat as he abused Kirill's asshole. Kirill wanted it. He wanted all of it and he was pretty sure he would die without them.

Before the last wave died away, the truth settled in. These men were one hundred percent his. All the times in his life that he had thought he had met someone special was nothing in comparison. His soul had been rocked. They completed him. It wasn't only the earth-shattering orgasm talking. He had met the pieces of his heart that had been missing his entire life. For the first time, Kirill felt whole. He never wanted this to end.

SEVEN

JETT TRAILED HIS FINGERS ALONG KIRILL'S dresser, learning about his man by inspecting his things. Three bottles of cologne sat beside a pocket watch. Jett picked up each bottle and sniffed. They all had the same underlying notes—cocoa and spice. Bold and beautiful—like the man. Jett popped open the pocket watch. A single word was inscribed inside.

Ours

A smile tugged at Jett's lips. He liked the idea of someone giving Kirill this watch in the name of love. Jett wanted all Kirill's stories, but Kirill acted—for the most part—like he never existed before meeting Derreck and him. In a way, that was sweet.

Unfortunately, it hindered Jett's ability to get as close as he wanted. Derreck, Jett understood him. He had been raised by a single mother. When Derreck had been fourteen, they had been evicted from their apartment and forced to live in their car. At sixteen, she had sent him inside a department store to buy bread and disappeared, abandoning him. He had fallen through the cracks of society. A hard shell had formed around Derreck's heart. Before Jett, only Antonio had scaled Derreck's walls. Derreck loved Jett, but he feared being abandoned even more, so—sometimes—Derreck destroyed things before they destroyed him. Jett genuinely believed this new relationship dynamic would be beneficial to Derreck's mental health. He could feel safe—like they were a family. But Kirill, Jett didn't know how to keep him. Kirill had this huge house and a powerful family. Jett wanted this relationship to be special to Kirill. He simply didn't know how to make it important to someone who didn't really let them in.

"Are you bored?"

Jett's eyes fell closed as Kirill's hands slid across his waist and Kirill's chest pressed against Jett's back. "No. I'm being nosy." Jett covered Kirill's hands with his, keeping Kirill in place. "I'm hoping I can uncover all your secrets and trick you into falling for me."

A sexy laugh vibrated against the shell of Jett's ear as Kirill kissed it. "Do you really want that? I'm possessive and jealous."

"Being possessive is an odd stance, considering."

"Oh, sexy," Kirill growled as he nipped at Jett's neck. "Make no mistake, Derreck is mine too. The three of us are a team, but if anyone else looks at either of you, you'll see a side of me you're likely to hate."

Kirill had no idea. His words stole Jett's breath. Jett needed to be fiercely wanted. "Promise? I've always been pretty easy to throw away."

"You'll see," Kirill said, skimming his lips across Jett's shoulder one more time. "Are you sure you won't come to the gym with Derreck and me?"

Jett snorted. "Are you saying I'm fat?"

Kirill released a tired-sounding sigh. "You know I'm not."

Jett bit back a laugh at Kirill's put-upon tone. "Go. I plan to snoop through your things and then lounge by the pool. You two need to get all sweaty and hard for me while I'm being lazy."

Derreck appeared in the doorway. "I wondered where you two had gone." He moved farther into the room. His gaze latched on to Jett. "Have you changed your mind about going with us?"

Jett rolled his eyes. "Definitely not. As much as I adore watching sexy men sweat, I get bored quickly and would rather watch you two sweating in private. So, go. Have fun."

With a smile, Derreck crossed the room. He wrapped his arms around Kirill and Jett. Derreck took turns kissing Jett's and Kirill's necks. "You're tempting me to stay, but I turn to jelly way too quickly to skip gym time. So enjoy your pool time, but put on sunscreen."

"Yes, sir. Love you."

Derreck kissed the tip of Jett's nose before linking fingers with Kirill and pulling away. "Love you too." His gaze slid Kirill's way. "Are you ready, sexy?"

Something passed over Kirill's features. It was gone too quickly for Jett to decipher. For a second, though, it almost looked as if Kirill was hurt. Jett's throat tightened in response. Kirill nodded at Derreck's question and they were gone before Jett recovered enough to speak out. He shook his head. A snort escaped him. Jett had no reason to believe Kirill was unhappy. With a sigh, he undressed.

Jett still didn't have anything to wear to the pool.

Not that anyone would see him. He shamelessly searched Kirill's cabinets and found sunscreen. By the time he was coated in lotion and had a beach towel around his hips, Jett had almost lost his desire to go swimming. Even though he was alone, Jett still laughed aloud. He was the only person he knew who dreaded doing nothing. His thoughts were usually too dark to be alone. Jett would deal. It was nice outside and he could relax. Kirill and Derreck wouldn't be gone forever. He would survive.

On the way to the back door, someone knocked on the front. Jett froze in his tracks. Surely if it was one of the guys, they had a way to get in. Unless they were back so soon because Kirill had forgotten his keys. Jett only wore a towel. He glanced down at himself and sighed. Fuck. He was nude underneath. With nothing for it, Jett changed directions and answered the door. The most beautiful man Jett had ever set eyes on stood on the other side. Jett blinked. His tongue froze to the roof of his mouth. The blond man had sky-blue eyes and perfect lips. They were so full, they practically begged for someone to suck them. His sexy gaze moved down Jett's body, making Jett fight the urge to cover himself.

Jett fought a blush. "Can I help you?"

The guy's gaze snapped back to Jett's face at the question. "Yeah. Is Ki home?"

For a moment, Jett simply blinked at the name until it occurred to him the dude probably meant Kirill. "I don't know who that is unless you're referring to Kirill."

A smile exploded across the guy's face. Jett nearly sighed. He had perfect teeth and adorable dimples. "Yes. Kirill. I'm Zach, by the way," Zach said, holding out his hand for Jett to shake.

Jett lightly shook before quickly releasing him. A horrible suspicion crept in now that Jett's initial shock had passed. "Jett. Kirill isn't home."

Zach's smile slipped away. "Oh. I ran into Pytor this morning and he said Kirill was in town."

Jett nodded. "He is, but he just left for the gym."

"Oh." Zach's expression shifted. He eyed Jett's half-dressed state again. Jett saw the exact moment Zach realized Jett was more than a friend. The way his features hardened confirmed Jett's thoughts. Zach considered himself more than a friend too.

Jett's discomfort had him becoming the pretender. He wrapped himself in an over-the-top cheerful facade to hide his heart. "I don't know how long he'll be gone, but I can definitely let him know you stopped by."

Zach matched Jett's fake smile. "I'll find him at the gym. We go to the same one. I'm surprised you didn't go with him," Zach tacked on while letting his gaze slide down Jett's body again.

That clinched it. Zach had a pretty face, but it masked a bitch. Jett's smile kicked up a notch. "I have a naturally thin physique. I don't have to work at it. Good luck in your search." Jett shut the door without saying goodbye or waiting for Zach to insult him again. After all, nothing Jett said topped the fact that Jett was the one freely staying in Kirill's house. Not Zach. Despite that inner pep talk, Jett still had a kernel of doubt eating away at him. They had established it was the three of them and no one else. Jett fucking hated the idea of anyone touching Kirill. Jett took a breath, hoping to calm his nerves. There was no reason not to trust Kirill until Kirill gave him one. That didn't stop Jett's chest from hurting. He might have made a mistake coming here. Jett supposed he would learn soon enough.

DERRECK DIDN'T NEED WHOEVER HE DATED TO also be his workout buddy. He would keep hitting the gym no matter what. After all, he had been going alone for years with no trouble. But he had to admit, it was nice having someone to spot him and tease him into doing more and more. His muscles screamed from the way Kirill challenged him to be better and try new things and from the full night of fucking everywhere they could. By the car ride home, Derreck's cheeks hurt from smiling. His chest felt full. There was never a time in Derreck's life that he could recall being this happy. Jett had come back to him. Kirill was making them better. A part of him didn't want to trust this newfound joy, but he couldn't stop getting sucked deeper.

Kirill glanced his way and smiled. "You look happy."

"I am." Derreck reached over and took Kirill's hand. Kirill didn't hesitate to link his fingers through Derreck's. Derreck brought their joined hands to his mouth. His brushed his lips across Kirill's hand. "Thank you."

"For what?"

Derreck didn't know where to start. "Everything. Bringing us here. Sharing yourself with us. Wanting me."

Kirill's gaze slid his way again. "You shouldn't be thanking me for any of that. I've been watching you for a while, you know?"

He had not known that. "Seriously?"

With his attention locked on the road, Kirill nodded. "You're incredibly sexy and you've always looked so sad. I've been fascinated. Meeting Jett felt like serendipity. Also, it felt like the curtain was pulled back and I finally saw the entire picture. You shouldn't thank me for taking a chance."

Derreck mulled over the confession before speaking his mind. "Yes, I should. Without you stepping in and taking control, I would've chosen to stay miserable forever. I fucked up with Jett. As you know, I kissed someone else behind his back after telling him that he was my whole world. No matter how nonsexual that kiss might've been, it undermined everything we were building. Without you, I would've chosen to continue taking my punishment for that mistake without trying again."

Kirill snorted. "As Jett has tried telling you, a kiss wouldn't break him. My impression is he was already broken when he met you. That kiss probably just broke whatever kept him from seeking help. Everything happens for a reason. If I hadn't come along, you two would've found another way back to each other."

Derreck couldn't let that idea stand. "Maybe, but this is better. I honestly believe, without you, we would always know we were missing something but never know that it's you."

Kirill glanced his way before quickly focusing on the road again. "Thank you for that. Sometimes I don't always know what I need to hear, but I needed to hear that."

Since Derreck had always been uncomfortable with praise, he immediately searched for a change in topic. He eyed the nice car they were in. It was a new Hellcat created to look like an old Charger. "I love this car, by the way. It's so odd to me that you have this whole life here in California. A gorgeous house and a nice car. It's like there're two of you. One here and one back home."

"Maybe there are two of me," Kirill said, surprising Derreck. "I just haven't decided which one to be yet."

Instead of feeling discouraged by Kirill's confession, Derreck's hopes were bolstered. "I think Jett and I can convince you to choose wisely."

"Maybe so," Kirill said with a smile as he pulled into the garage. They headed inside hand in hand before parting ways inside the kitchen. Derreck went on the hunt for Jett. He found him the first place he looked. Jett was sound asleep on his stomach on a lounge chair by the pool. Derreck sat sideways on the lounge beside Jett and stared at him in silence. He knew he should wake Jett and get him out of the sun, but Jett looked peaceful. The sight of his perfect spine called to Derreck. Derreck leaned closer and pressed his lips to Jett's back. Jett startled so hard that Derreck almost felt guilty.

Jett eyed Derreck for a moment, visibly struggling with that first moment of confusion that came with waking up in a strange place.

Derreck smiled. "Hey, sweet angel. Did you enjoy your nap?"

Jett rolled and stretched, giving Derreck's eyes a feast. "*Mhmm.* How was the gym?"

"Pretty amazing, actually. It wasn't a regular gym. They had like climbing walls and whatnot. It was a lot of fun."

Jett sat up, wincing as if he had slept wrong. "Did Zach find Kirill?"

Derreck's forehead furrowed. "Who?"

While rearranging his towel to cover his junk, Jett kept his gaze locked on his task. "Zach. He stopped by while you were gone."

"Did you tell him to go fuck himself?" Kirill said behind Derreck.

Derreck glanced over as Kirill dropped down next to Derreck on the lounge. Kirill handed them ice cold bottles of water while waiting for Jett's response.

Jett didn't meet anyone's gaze as he cracked open the bottle. "Thanks," he muttered beneath his breath before taking a sip.

Kirill didn't back down. "You didn't answer my question."

Jett's gaze finally slid Kirill's way. "I didn't, but I did practically slam the door in his face after he insinuated that I'm fat and should've gone to the gym with you."

Derreck blinked. He would find this Zach guy and kill him. Not only did Jett not have an ounce of fat on his body, but Jett had also been bullied and beaten his entire life. This Zach guy really needed to die.

"That sounds like Zach."

The bitter edge to Kirill's tone had Derreck's attention. "Who is this guy?"

Jett's gaze sharpened—like he wanted to know the answer too.

Kirill shrugged. "Just an ex. Definitely no one to worry about. How do you two feel about a trip to the grocery store? We could grab some steaks and fire up the grill tonight."

It couldn't have been more obvious Kirill didn't

want to discuss Zach. Derreck's gaze slid Jett's way. They shared a look and silent conversation. They would let this drop.

Jett smiled. "That sounds great. Just let me grab a quick shower and we'll go."

Derreck and Kirill both stood so fast, they nearly bumped heads as they jumped to their feet. "I'll join you," they said simultaneously before sharing a wicked smile.

Jett chuckled as he stood. "I believe we've established there's room for all three of us in Kirill's gigantic shower."

Derreck and Kirill shared another lecherous smile as they followed Jett inside. They were sweaty and gross, but they could get clean while getting dirty. Derreck had a feeling this weekend would ruin his ability to ever shower alone again. After all, he had never realized how much he had been missing.

EIGHT

With only a half day scheduled at work, Kirill couldn't wait to be done, and alone with his men. His mood was like the relationship equivalent of spring fever. By the time Derreck and Kirill were headed out, Kirill was practically running to his Jeep. They had nothing planned for the night beyond—finally—taking Jett the things he had left at Derreck's when they had split. Still, Kirill couldn't wait.

Derreck chuckled at his over-enthusiasm to be free. "I've never seen anyone so excited to move and unpack boxes."

Kirill shrugged. "What can I say? The thought of spending the night unpacking boxes with Jett and you is better than doing anything at all with anyone else."

The happiness in Derreck's expression made his confession worthwhile. All the way to Derreck's house, Kirill toyed with Derreck's fingers and dreamed. They had been seeing each other for four months now. Kirill could say without bias that being with Jett and Derreck was fucking amazing. While they occasionally had disagreements, they had gotten pretty good at resolving things through ridiculous methods—like a coin toss and rock, paper, scissors. There were only two points of contention that couldn't be resolved that way. Jett absolutely refused to go to Derreck's place, and Kirill was having a much harder time than he expected adjusting to the pair loving each other but not him. Jett and Derreck only knew about one of those issues. Under no circumstances could Kirill confess to being bothered by the pair's exclusive I love yous. Just the thought made Kirill feel weak. They didn't have to give him any affection, but they did. Kirill was scared shitless they would never love him too.

At Derreck's house, Kirill couldn't stop watching Derreck's every move. He really was gorgeous. It wasn't just his looks that Kirill couldn't resist. Derreck had an inner beauty. Everything he did, taking extra care of everyone, showed how much he valued the people in his life. Derreck didn't expect a single thing from anyone else. He took care of everything. Derreck cooked, cleaned, always made sure everyone ate and slept. He opened doors and ran errands. No one asked. Derreck simply took care of everything, showing his love through actions. Kirill had never been with anyone like him. His attention sucked Kirill in a little more every day, making him realize he would never be happy with anyone else the way he was in this relationship.

Kirill followed Derreck from room to room as he gathered Jett's things and ensured he hadn't forgotten anything. As Derreck made a final sweep of the house, Kirill stalked him. The small two-bedroom house didn't offer many places for Derreck to escape. The desire to touch Derreck built by the second. He couldn't take another second of staring at Derreck's ass. Before Derreck could escape back to the Jeep, Kirill pounced. He leapt in front of Derreck and closed the door.

Laughing amber eyes focused on him. "Nice reflexes. All that extra working out is really showing. But you're still not quick enough," Derreck said, snagging Kirill around the waist and lifting his feet from the floor. Kirill wasn't a small guy. He was average height and weight, but Derreck tossed Kirill over his shoulder like he weighed nothing. His palm collided with Kirill's ass, making Kirill squirm. He didn't stop with one blow. Laughter had Kirill's entire body shaking and no air reached his brain. Before he could think of a way to recover, Derreck tossed Kirill on the couch and covered Kirill's body with his. Their mouths clashed as they fought to get closer. They always exploded into an inferno when they were alone. Kirill was already so hard, he couldn't breathe. Then Derreck's weight shifted until he held Kirill so lovingly that Kirill's eyes stung. Sometimes, at the most unexpected moments, when he was with Jett and Derreck, Kirill felt overwhelmed and loved. It was nearly crippling. His heart didn't know how to have them but not really have them. Jett and Derreck were the real couple. They might have opened their relationship to Kirill, but he wasn't a part of them. Not really. But moments like these, being held, caressed, and petted, Kirill's brain felt tricked by the touches. He had never wanted anything like he wanted this.

Derreck's phone chirped. "That would be Jett. He's waiting for us," Derreck whispered against Kirill's lips, bringing him back to reality. Sometimes, Kirill was torn down the middle. He wanted to confess his love and beg Jett and Derreck to give him the same. Other times, he recognized how lucky he was to have them at all. He was scared to lose them by making demands. After all, having some of them was better than nothing. Wasn't it? Kirill didn't know anymore.

———

THEY HAD FALLEN INTO A PATTERN. KIRILL tweaked the schedule, ensuring Derreck and he could ride to and from work together each day. They also had the same days off. Jett made sure he was home every day before they arrived. Derreck never asked Jett to come to his place. Jett appreciated that more than Derreck would ever know. Even though they had made their new relationship dynamic work for four months and Jett was happier than he had ever been in his life, Jett still felt funny about Derreck's house. Jett had lived there once upon a time. He had abandoned a life there, clothes and all. Every time he thought about the place, he felt a panic attack rise. It wasn't like anything bad had ever happened there. Jett had simply left his old self there. Nothing scared him more than becoming who he used to be. He had an irrational fear of opening Derreck's door and finding his old self waiting. He liked the new them better, but he knew eventually he would have to face the past again. So Jett decided to start small. He had Derreck bring back the boxes filled with the things he had left behind.

"Oh, goddamn." Kirill snatched up a leather thong that had a matching collar from the first box Jett opened. "Put this on. I want to see."

With a hot blush, Jett snagged the wisp of material and shoved it inside the bedside table. "It probably doesn't fit anymore."

Derreck cast Kirill a laughing glance. "He's still the same size, and yes, it's every bit as hot as you're picturing."

Kirill released a sexy growl that weakened Jett's knees. "You will wear that for me one day."

Jett bit back a smile. "Maybe."

A wickedness tinted Kirill's features that made it even harder for Jett to keep standing. Kirill reclined on the bed and eyed Jett's body. "I'll do all the things to you if you try it on right now."

Something about Kirill's words and tone brought a completely random memory from the depths of Jett's brain. His gaze shot to Derreck's. They shared a mischievous smile before chanting at the same time, "Do you want to do some sex or..." They burst into laughter.

Kirill looked between them. "What the fuck was that?"

Jett shook his head and swiped at his eyes as the chuckles dried away. "Goddamn. That feels like so long ago. We used to watch this hilarious web show. I haven't thought it about in a long time. That's a thing one of the characters used to say. Something about your offer sounded exactly like that character, saying, 'Do you want to do some sex, or...'"

An odd look passed over Kirill's features. For a moment, he almost looked sad before turning his head. "Sounds like an interesting show."

"What's wrong?" Jett felt like Kirill hid something and it twisted Jett's heart.

Kirill focused on Jett again. The hint of sadness was gone. "Nothing." He shook his head. A sweet smile touched his lips. "You two are so much in love and in sync that it hits me anew sometimes. It's beautiful to watch."

Derreck moved to stand behind Jett. He pressed his lips to Jett's ear, and whispered, stopping Jett from responding. "I think Kirill feels neglected. You should try on the leather outfit and remind him that he's a part of us too."

Even though he knew he was being manipulated, Jett's lips stretched into a smile. He wouldn't let

Kirill feel neglected. Jett peeled off his shirt. Derreck opened the drawer Jett had shoved the costume into. Kirill's gaze sharpened. With his shirt gone, Jett stood still while Derreck snapped the collar around his throat. He felt the weight of it changing him, making him meek yet powerful. Jett would do whatever they asked, but he also knew the truth. He was the one in charge.

With his collar in place, Jett stripped away the rest of his clothing. Before he could put on the leather thong, Kirill stopped him. "You can forgo the rest of the outfit. I want you nude."

Jett's cock stirred at the words. He liked being wanted. No one understood how much. Derreck moved the box Jett had been unpacking from the bed. Kirill settled onto his back. He crooked his finger at Jett. Jett immediately complied. He crawled onto the bed. Jett moved slow, letting Kirill's anticipation grow. His gaze snapped to Kirill's jeans as Kirill went to work on the front of his pants. Saliva filled Jett's mouth as Kirill's cock sprang from his jeans.

"Suck it, Jett."

Even though there was nothing sweet about Kirill's demand, Jett was already too turned on to scoff. Still, he glanced over his shoulder to find Derreck stripping.

Derreck gave him a subtle nod. "Lock those sexy lips around his dick, Jett. You know I like to watch."

With Derreck's permission, Jett lowered his head. He kissed a thick vein that ran the length of Kirill's erection. Kirill's eyes already looked desperate as he stared down the line of his body. Jett swallowed a laugh. Kirill didn't even realize Jett was the one in control. He flicked his tongue, teasing the soft skin that stretched Kirill's hard cock. Kirill hissed. His hips left the bed. A drop of pre-cum escaped Jett's erection. The bed dipped as Derreck joined them. Derreck fisted Kirill's dick and held it upright so they could tongue kiss their man's cock while stealing kisses from each other. Their heated gazes collided with Kirill's erection between them. Jett felt the promise in Derreck's eyes. He would get fucked hard after this. Jett felt it in his soul, and he couldn't wait.

———

EVEN WITH TWO MEN ON HIS DICK, AND TURNED on past insanity, there was still a truth growing in Kirill's brain. His time was up here. In the past four months, he had watched their inside jokes grow. Kirill had listened to the whispered I love yous. He had fought hard not to feel left out. They were beautiful. Kirill loved them, and that was the problem. He was—once again—wasting his love on a couple that would never love him in return. If Kirill stayed, forcing them to tell him goodbye, that might break them. Their love was gorgeous yet fragile and Kirill couldn't be the reason they didn't bloom.

That heartbreaking knowledge muted as he watched Jett crawl up his body. Their lips met. It was impossible to think of losing this with Jett's tongue stroking his. With his mind distracted by the sweet and sexy kiss, his breath was easily stolen when the tight heat of Jett's body squeezed his dick. The breathing issue got worse when Derreck joined them. Derreck fingered the same asshole that already sucked on Kirill's cock. The extra lube he added was cold compared to Jett's heat. Kirill held still and let everything happen to him. He couldn't stop kissing Jett. Kirill was almost desperate for the taste of Jett's tongue. Then the unthinkable occurred. Derreck's huge cock joined his inside Jett.

A loud gasp ripped from Kirill's throat. The tight fit was almost painful. Jett threw his head back and cried out. The muscles straining in his pale neck looked fragile with the black leather and silver studded collar embracing it. Kirill swore the world stopped turning as Jett's body tried sucking them deeper. Hot cum flooded the space between their bodies. Oxygen seemed to disappear from the room as everything narrowed to a pinpoint. Kirill's entire being focused on the pleasure of his dick. A moan tore from him as an orgasm struck like lightning. While he shook from the power of the moment, the painful truth re-emerged. This wasn't his life. It was theirs. Kirill was just a temporary visitor. He could either hang around until he broke them or he could do everything within his power to ensure they had a perfect and secure future. He would do the latter. Kirill loved them too much to consider anything else.

Even as Derreck collapsed and gasped for air, he felt a change in the room. He couldn't explain his sudden surety that something was wrong. Then Jett kissed him, and the feeling passed. Multiple chimes cut through the air, making Derreck groan. Kirill had a wretched text alert tone that couldn't be mistaken for anyone else's phone. Derreck imagined that was exactly why he kept it.

Derreck rolled, setting Kirill free to check his messages, since they wouldn't stop coming in. He stared at Kirill's profile as Kirill stared at his phone. The light from the device made the man's features seem harsher than usual. With a growl, Kirill rolled and sat up.

"Goddamn it. I have to head back to work. A drunken brawl broke out inside the nightclub at Luna East. Two of the front windows were busted out. Six people have been arrested and countless guests are demanding their money back for their stay."

Jett rubbed his back. "Poor angel. Always the levelheaded one who takes control."

Kirill pressed a quick kiss to Jett's lips before focusing on Derreck. "I'll arrange for someone to pick you up for work in the morning. I don't know how long this will take."

Something about Kirill's tone didn't feel right. It didn't sound real. "Do you need me to come with you? Things might go quicker with both of us there."

Kirill shook his head. "Jett needs you more. He deserves to be babied after our rough treatment."

Derreck couldn't argue with that. They had never really discussed taking Jett at the same time like that. Derreck had gotten carried away. "Okay.

Call me if you change your mind. I can Uber over there or whatever."

Kirill leaned in and kissed Derreck. It was sweet and lingering—like a proper goodbye. Derreck couldn't shake the feeling of wrongness. Maybe Kirill was right, though. It was possible he just felt guilty for taking Jett as hard as he had.

Derreck pulled away and kissed the tip of Kirill's nose. "Be careful going back to work. I'll see you in the morning."

With a nod, Kirill dropped his head and kissed Jett again. He whispered something Derreck didn't catch before rolling away and leaving them behind.

Derreck dropped his chin and eyed Jett. His cheeks were flushed, but he didn't look any worse for the wear. "Are you okay?"

Jett nodded.

Derreck couldn't let it go. He grabbed the covers and snuggled beneath them with Jett in his arms. "Are you sure? I didn't ask for your permission before going all in like that."

Jett chuckled. His body shook with silent laughter. "Did you hear me complaining?"

"No, but still."

Jett shushed him and kissed him so he couldn't talk anymore. His emotions settled down. Some of his fear slipped away. "I love you," Derreck whispered against Jett's lips, because he couldn't stop.

"I love you too."

With Jett's reassurances and words of love brushing his skin, Derreck let the cares of the world slip away. As much as he wished the three of them could be snuggling right now, after having his world rocked, one of the things Derreck loved most about Kirill was his capability. He was strong and steady. Dependable. Derreck didn't doubt for a second that Kirill would smooth things over quickly and be back in bed with them before the end of the night. He didn't think Kirill could stand an empty bed at the hotel—not when Jett and Derreck were right here waiting. He would be back. Derreck believed in him.

NINE

THERE WAS A HOLLOW PIT IN DERRECK'S GUT. Kirill hadn't come back last night and wasn't answering his texts today. Derreck had gotten to work fifteen minutes early, hoping to hunt him down. While Kirill hadn't done or said anything to make Derreck think there was a problem per se, Derreck felt the same way he had when Jett had abandoned him a year earlier. It was entirely possible that Derreck had some issues and there was nothing to worry about. Derreck needed to set eyes on Kirill. He wouldn't feel better until Kirill told him they were fine.

After ten minutes of searching all the obvious places, Derreck gave up and stopped at the first craps table he came to. Marla, a longtime employee, manned the table. Since it was early and the casino was dead, she looked bored.

She perked up at the sight of him. "Hey, Derreck. How are you this morning?"

Derreck's anxiety kept him from making small talk. "I'm good. Have you seen Kirill around?"

Marla leaned closer—like she didn't want to be overheard. "Zander Kapra showed up here this morning. I heard a rumor that Kirill has left his position and Zander is here to deal with the empty slot." She winked. "My money is on you getting the job."

Derreck couldn't breathe. Kirill left. Where had he gone? What the actual fuck? He couldn't show his panic, since no one knew they were together, but goddamn. Kirill was gone. Derreck didn't understand.

Marla's smile disappeared. "Heads up. Mafia goon closing in." She quickly turned away and pretended to work, leaving Derreck to deal with the behemoth bearing down on him. He pinned Derreck in place with his intense stare. "Mr. Kapra would like a moment of your time."

Derreck pasted on his best customer service smile. "Of course." With his agreement in place, Derreck pretended to have a choice in the matter as he followed the guy to the elevator. The ride up to the penthouse was made in heavy silence. Derreck fought the urge to chatter nervously while his thoughts still raced around Kirill. How could Kirill just leave? Derreck couldn't believe this was happening again.

When the elevator doors opened, his dark-haired companion motioned for Derreck to step out first. Derreck glanced around as he moved away from the elevator. When Antonio had lived here, the penthouse looked like a home. Now it looked like a giant office. A shirtless and gorgeous man with huge cut muscles walked by, drying his hair with a towel. He didn't even look Derreck's way. Derreck couldn't stop his eyes from following the guy as he disappeared inside the bedroom.

"That's my husband, Maverick," a voice said from behind the desk. Derreck's gaze swung that way, fighting a blush. He hadn't meant to ogle Kapra's husband. Zander Kapra was even sexier, making Derreck wonder if everyone in the Kapra family was beautiful. Derreck had never actually met Zander, but Derreck knew it was him at first sight. His entire demeanor screamed power. His eerily light blue eyes stayed locked on Derreck as Derreck crossed the room.

Deciding to gloss over checking out the man's husband, Derreck decided to go with the obvious. "Your..." His gaze slid the guard's way. "... assistant said you needed to see me."

Zander quickly pulled his shoulder-length blond hair into a messy bun. "Yes, thank you, Pytor," Zander said absently before focusing on Derreck again. "My driver, Yaro, is on his way to pick up Jett and will meet you at the airstrip."

Derreck rocked back on his heels and cleared his throat as he tried to decide what in the hell was going on. "Um, okay. Why?"

Zander leaned forward and set his elbows on the desk. His stare was too intense for Derreck to look anywhere else. "Do you love Kirill or this job?"

Derreck froze. He didn't know how to respond. Zander was the top boss. Kirill and Derreck were both managers. Derreck wasn't sure what answer Zander expected to hear.

"I assure you I'm not trying to trick you. It's a simple question."

Derreck needed this job, but at the end of the day, Kirill mattered more. "If I have to choose, then Kirill."

Zander nodded. "Good. Now, the time has come to

make him see it. Kirill went back to California last night and asked me to promote you to general manager." Rage had Derreck's blood pressure shooting through the roof. Kirill had fucking left them. He had left without a word —like everyone Derreck had ever loved. Zander eyed him in silence for a moment. A loud sigh finally escaped Zander. "You really don't see it, do you?"

At the current moment, Derreck didn't see anything but his rising temper. "See what?" No matter how he tried to hide it, Derreck's rage showed in his biting tone.

Zander shook his head. A small smile touched his lips. "I will tell you something no one knows. Kirill isn't really my cousin. The streets raised us in a country where the streets were beyond cold. We are blood in all the ways that truly matter. He is my cousin by pain and circumstance. You understand this."

Derreck nodded even as he tried to wade his way through Zander's non-explanation. He understood loving someone like family because they were there when all family disappeared. What Derreck didn't understand was what this had to do with Kirill's disappearance.

Zander didn't make him dig. "I think you also

know, when no one has ever loved you, how easy it is to believe you are unlovable."

"I do," Derreck confirmed. The more Zander spoke, the tighter Derreck's throat became. He understood the gist of things. Kirill had left, thinking he was unloved, while also showing his love by asking for Derreck's promotion. "When do I leave?"

Zander chuckled. "Now you sound like a man who deserves him. Pytor will take you. Don't worry about things here. I've been running Luna for many, many years. Things will still move smoothly while you are away."

Derreck had a hard time breathing, but he didn't let that fact slow him. He didn't give a fuck about the Luna, but he appreciated Zander. "Thank you. I'll fix this."

Zander had obviously already dismissed Derreck. His gaze was locked on his desk. "I know." With that affirmation hanging between them, Derreck headed for the elevator without waiting to see if Pytor followed. He had a relationship to save. There was no time to waste.

All the way to the airstrip, silence filled the car. Derreck's mind didn't exactly race. Neither was it silent. The same words chanted over and over again inside his head. Kirill couldn't leave. He was one part of them. They were a team of soul mates. Kirill couldn't leave. As Derreck stepped on to what appeared to be the same plane they had taken to California last time, he spotted Jett already onboard. Tears filled Jett's eyes the moment he saw Derreck. Derreck rushed to hold him. As Derreck's arms closed around Jett, a small, stuttered breath escaped Jett that broke Derreck's heart.

"We won't let him slip away."

Jett gave a tiny nod but still argued. "He's already gone. I don't understand. What did I do wrong?"

Derreck's eyes burned. His arms tightened around Jett. "You didn't do anything. Kirill has something going on inside his head that he's been keeping to himself. It's time for him to talk to us, but no way in hell is he allowed to disappear. Whatever it takes, we'll be there for him."

"Okay."

Jett didn't make another sound the entire flight. Derreck was too busy mulling over every second they had spent with Kirill to make small talk. He honestly didn't think Jett had done anything wrong, but Derreck couldn't be positive that he hadn't done something. Maybe Derreck had ruined them. Zander had claimed Kirill believed he was unlovable. Did that mean Derreck had made him feel unloved? He didn't know. All Derreck knew was they couldn't be over. Derreck wasn't ready to break again. He had to save them. Whatever it took. He had to make this right.

KIRILL WENT TO THE GYM BECAUSE THAT WAS what he always did. He had pulled into the parking lot, parked in the first space he came to, and immediately spotted Zach's car. For several minutes, Kirill stared at the Dodge Charger he had helped buy. Zach hadn't been taking care of it. It was dirty and the tires looked old. Zach never cared for things the way he should—Kirill included.

Even after killing the engine, Kirill couldn't convince himself to go inside. His heart ached. Seeing Zach would only make things worse. Kirill wasn't strong enough to face all the things he had lost in the last couple of years. Kirill didn't miss Zach anymore. He never even thought about the guy. But losing Jett and Derreck was fresh and Zach would be like acid on that open wound. So Kirill restarted his engine and headed back home.

Eventually, Kirill would need to make a plan. He

couldn't live without a job. The best thing to do would be to sell his house. He could live off that profit for a while. It would at least hold him over until he found another job. Being unemployed was worth it, as long as Derreck got that promotion and could give Jett and himself a great life, Kirill would be fine. He could live with anything as long as they were good. With Kirill out of the way, they could get married. Buy a house. Get a dog. He hoped they had a beautiful future. Kirill knew his leaving had been abrupt. Likely, they wouldn't understand. But each and every moment Kirill had spent with them, he had done so knowing that he was the intruder—just as he had been in Tim and Zach's marriage. Kirill couldn't stand being the third wheel any longer. It was best to go while all the memories were still beautiful.

Back home, as soon as Kirill let himself inside, he knew. He felt them. Kirill's pace picked up as his feet carried him toward the men who owned his heart. Derreck sat in the oversized chair in the living room with Jett in his lap. They looked devastated. Kirill could barely breathe. "You're here." God help him. He couldn't stop the words from bursting from him. No one had ever chased after him. Neither man flinched at the sound of

Kirill's voice. Their broken expressions didn't waver.

"You left us." Derreck's voice sounded gravelly. Guilt set in.

"You two have each other." Fuck. Kirill didn't know what else to say as he moved to stand over them. He had left them. Kirill had done that. What had he been thinking?

An adorable line appeared between Jett's eyebrows. "What's that supposed to mean? We have you too. Or, at least, I thought we did until you just left. No warning. Just gone."

Kirill couldn't stop a sad smile from touching his lips. Jett was sweet. Kirill's gaze moved between the two men who had stolen his heart. Derreck's dark expression screamed he was pissed about having to chase after Kirill. A smile exploded across Kirill's face. He really did love these men. This hurt like hell, but he knew from experience it would hurt even more if he forced them to tell him goodbye. "I don't want to become the love-blocking asshole in your lives."

"What?" Derreck practically barked the question, as if daring Kirill to continue down this path. "Explain."

There was no turning back. Kirill took a breath,

trying to squelch the pain. He sat on the footstool in front of them, set his elbows on his knees, and dove in. "You two loved each other before I came around. Maybe I kind of helped you with getting back together, but we all know it's only a matter of time before I'm asked to move along." Kirill took another deep breath and focused on the couple. "I'm the odd man out here. It's best I see you two as the blessing you've been and get out of the way before I get my heart broken again."

Derreck shifted Jett onto one knee before leaning forward and tugging Kirill into his lap too. "Okay. You say 'again' like we've broken your heart in the past. Tell us what's going on in your head."

Kirill didn't respond right away. It felt too good in Derreck's lap. Kirill turned sideways and cuddled up. Derreck was so big, he had no trouble holding Jett and Kirill at the same time. Jett smiled like he knew Kirill's thoughts. They were needy when it came to cuddles, but Derreck had enough to give.

The pains in Kirill's chest said he needed to explain and move along before being with them killed him. He took a breath and told the story he never wanted to tell. "This isn't my first relationship like this one." Once the first words were out there, the rest of the story poured from him—like he had been waiting for someone to ask. "When I met Tim and Zach, they had been together seven years and married for three. We clicked immediately and started doing everything together. If they went to dinner, I went too. Everything. I was always the third wheel, but I didn't feel like it." Kirill kept his gaze locked on Jett. Jett looked so understanding that Kirill couldn't stop confessing everything. "To this day, I don't understand how I ended up in their bed. I just did. Then, it didn't stop. They kind of moved in with me while I wasn't looking, and we settled into a life together. I loved them." Kirill took a breath. He still felt like such a goddamn idiot.

"It's okay," Jett said, taking his hand.

A sad smile touched Kirill's lips. He knew Jett understood humiliation. That gave him the strength to tell the rest. "One day, I came home, and they were packed to leave. They said all the things you'd expect. It had been fun. They needed to get back to concentrating on each other. Surely there were no hard feelings because I had to have known they would want to start a real family one day. Oh, and thanks for letting us crash here while we saved money for a new place." Kirill blinked. His eyes burned. "I was completely in love with them and I was just a good time. Fucking me was how they lived rent free."

"Oh, sweetie." Jett leaned forward and pressed his lips to Kirill's in a quick kiss. "Surely you don't think things are like that with us."

Kirill couldn't lie. "I don't, but I didn't think things were like that with them either. All I know is, you two already loved each other before I came along. I don't think I can survive hearing you two tell me I'm just a good time. So I'll duck out now and let you build your life."

Jett blew out a breath and looked Derreck's way. "Do you want to go first?"

Derreck gave a sharp nod and focused on Kirill. As always, his intensity made Kirill hold his breath. "I love you. This isn't Jett's and my relationship." Derreck took turns kissing Kirill's and Jett's shoulders. "This is *our* relationship. The three of us. Together. If you're choosing to leave us, you're choosing to break our hearts, and I demand a better excuse than two assholes once broke your heart. Everyone has baggage. Only fucking liars claim they don't. But I thought the three of us had already chosen each other. If I'm doing something that makes you feel like the odd man out, fucking say it so I can change. But don't break my heart for something I didn't do."

Kirill flinched at the harshness in Derreck's tone. He looked at Jett, hoping for a softer fall. Instead, Jett gave him a sharp nod. "What he said. I love you. If you plan to leave me, I want to hear what I did to deserve it. Not what fucking Zach did. The son of a bitch already called me fat. Don't break my heart for him."

Kirill looked between them. He didn't know what to say. In all the time he had been with Tim and Zach, they had never exchanged I love yous. After they were over, Kirill had recognized all the signs he had missed. He had felt like a fool. Still did. Jett and Derreck were right, though. He shouldn't punish them for someone else's sins, especially since Derreck and Jett claimed they loved him. No one else had ever given him that.

"I want to watch that web show with you." Damn. Kirill hated the neediness in his voice. He was being ridiculous. They would always have memories that didn't include him. Inside jokes he would always be on the outside of, because they had known each other longer. Kirill immediately backpedaled. "Never mind. Ignore that. I shouldn't be jealous of the time you were together without me."

Derreck kissed his forehead. "Stop. We would love to share our love of ridiculous shows with you."

Jett nodded. "Also, I think we should just throw out the rest of the boxes Derreck brought over without unpacking them."

Now Kirill felt really dumb. "No. Seriously. I'm just being extra sensitive or whatever. I really loved the collar and I'm sure there're more fun things waiting to tempt me in those boxes."

Jett sat up and dropped his gaze. He stared at his hands as he twisted his fingers in his lap. "I know that neither of you really understands, but I need to throw those boxes away." Krill's throat hurt as he watched Jett physically struggle with whatever they couldn't see. "Just like I haven't been able to bring myself to go to Derreck's place, I can't handle those boxes being in my apartment." His chest expanded as he took a deep breath. Jett's chin lifted. Kirill's breath left his lungs in a whoosh. Jett's eyes were filled with tears and he looked ready to break. "I loved last night. I don't want either of you to think differently." Jett looked between them, as if pleading with them to understand. "But when I woke up this morning, those boxes were sitting there just taunting me with things I don't want to remember." He focused on Derreck. "When I disappeared from your life, I was completely broken. It was rock bottom for me. I either had to let Bay get me help or kill myself. Things were too dark inside me."

Kirill fought a wave of tears that threatened to spill over his lashes. He swore he physically felt Jett's pain.

Jett sniffed and took an audible breath. He looked between them. "I don't know if it's PTSD like my counselor claims I have, or some sort of fucked up pain association, but I feel sick at the thought of opening any more of those boxes. This new me is better. I have to hang on to it."

"Derreck and I will throw them away," Kirill said without having to think about it. He had to act. Kirill couldn't let Jett keep ripping his own heart out just to explain himself to them. "You don't even have to look at them again. We'll take care of it."

"Damn right," Derreck said, backing him up.

A smile small hovered on Jett's lips as Jett swiped at his cheeks. "I love you both so much. I'm sorry you fell for such a mess."

Derreck snorted. "That's bullshit."

Kirill still felt the need to act. He had to fix everything. That was who he was. Plus, he needed to share the good thoughts he had been having before the dark thoughts had won, taking him away. "I want to buy us a house." Jett and Derreck looked his way. Certainty solidified inside him at their shocked expressions. He gave them a sharp nod. "It's time for me to sell this place and give up this town. Unless you two would like to live here," Kirill rushed to add. "Otherwise, let's sell it and buy a place together in Vegas."

"Really?" Jett sounded so hopeful. "I'd prefer to stay in Vegas, because I love my job. But are you really finally going to give up this town for us?"

Kirill nodded. "You two are all I care about. I want us to have our own place where we make new and happy memories. A place where none of us can run away again."

They looked Derreck's way. He was the only one who hadn't agreed. Derreck wore a huge grin. "I can't leave Vegas. Antonio and Bay are moving back to be closer to us."

Jett covered his mouth for a second before happiness burst out. "Are you fucking serious? I just talked to Bay the other day. He didn't say a word."

Derreck winced. "It's supposed to be a surprise."

Kirill didn't really know these people, but they

were important to Derreck and Jett. "So, I'm selling, then?"

Jett and Derreck looked his way and nodded. Derreck was the one who answered for them. "Let's do this. Let's create our own version of a family."

Kirill nearly collapsed under the weight of his relief and happiness. He stared at the loves of his life with his heart in his throat. While he had hoped for this, he had never dreamed he would have what Derreck and Jett offered with their love. He couldn't wait to get started. They were his whole world.

JETT FELT KIND OF CRAPPY AND EXPOSED DESPITE winning Kirill and them deciding to buy a house together. It wasn't anyone's fault. He had worked so hard to build himself anew and confessing to what those goddamn boxes had done to his sanity left him feeling slightly defeated. He found himself incapable of meeting anyone's stare, in spite of it being one the happiest moments of his life.

"You're so strong."

Jett's gaze shot to Kirill's at the words.

Kirill held his stare as if he could read Jett's mind. Jett swallowed the desire to cry again. Kirill didn't back down. "Seriously," Kirill said, pushing on. "You've survived." He linked fingers with Jett. "You survived for us. I truly believe that. You're not weak. In fact, you're the strongest person I know. Don't think about it anymore. If you can't stop, tell us so we can fix it. Okay? You're not alone."

Since Jett's throat hurt too badly to speak, he nodded. He swallowed past the lump in his throat, forcing words past his lips. "I love you so much. So much. I didn't mean to rain on our moment."

Derreck squeezed Jett and Kirill to his chest. "No one is ruining anything. This is our moment to say everything we've avoided or assumed we each knew. I've never been prouder. It's like we're real adults. It only took me forty years to get here."

A genuine smile pulled at Jett's lips. He had to admit he did feel pretty adult like. It was good. He felt strong. They felt strong. "*Mhmm*, well." He nuzzled Derreck's chest while toying with Kirill's fingers. "What do three very adult-like people do when they're in love and celebrating?"

Kirill shot forward and claimed Jett's lips. He pulled Derreck into their kiss. Jett's heart raced as their tongues stroked and they fought to get closer. As fast as it started, it was over. Kirill jumped to his feet.

"Adults order dinner, drink beer, and binge watch a web series."

With a laugh, Jett found a more comfortable spot on Derreck's lap. "Sparkling water for me, please." He liked this plan. An entire night curled up together, eating, laughing and enjoying one another. Jett couldn't think of anything better. Except maybe spending the rest of his life doing this. Jett needed that. He needed this. They were strong. They would make it.

TEN

PACKING WAS GOING SO MUCH SMOOTHER THAN Derreck imagined. Of course, that was helped greatly by Kirill's relationship with Zander. Zander had given them two weeks off with pay while they dealt with Kirill's move. The house had sold way faster than anyone anticipated. Derreck had a sneaking suspicion Zander was behind that too. Kirill hired a moving company to deal with Derreck's place and Jett's apartment. The contents of this house would be right behind Jett's and Derreck's things, but they had agreed together to go through everything and decide what to keep from the house in California. Plus, they felt a little connected to this place where they had only spent two long weekends together. They had been great weekends, though.

The first, they had agreed they were a throuple. The second, they had confessed their love. This house, in a town where Derreck had never lived, felt like a piece of them. It deserved a proper send off before they settled into their cozy three-bedroom home less than ten miles from work.

"I don't know how we'll fit three people's worth of kitchen stuff in one kitchen."

At Jett's observation, Kirill shrugged. "I say we just pack everything, get it home, and then donate whatever we don't need to charity."

Derreck nodded. "I like this plan. We can just keep what we like best. There's no need for this to become a thing—like trying to figure out who has the best bed did."

Kirill and Jett groaned, making Derreck chuckle. They had deteriorated to rock, paper, scissors to decide which bed would go in their bedroom. Jett had won and he had chosen the bed from this place. Honestly, it was the best decision for them. Still, Derreck would like to win occasionally. The doorbell rang, distracting him.

Derreck headed for the door. "That's probably the guy with the moving truck."

"Or the guy who's driving Kirill's car to Vegas," Jett pointed out helpfully.

Derreck flashed him a smile. He looked freaking adorable today, wearing flannel and with a bandanna covering his hair. Jett dove into everything with both feet. Even his house-packing clothing style. With a smile stretching his lips due to the happiness overflowing his heart, Derreck opened the door. Two blonds with matching Abercrombie shirts and haircuts stood on the other side. They had blue eyes. Both of them. They were damn near interchangeable. Derreck looked between them. "We're not looking to buy into any religion here." His gaze slid between them again. They gave him the creeps. "Or join any cults," he added for good measure.

The smaller of the two guys rolled his eyes. "We're looking for Ki. Just run along and get him. The help isn't supposed to be rude."

Derreck's tongue automatically ran across his teeth. He hadn't been to jail in over twenty years. Today, he might make an exception. Jett appeared at his side before Derreck knocked out a racist twat. "Hey, Bear, do I need to start taping…" Jett's words died away as he stared at the pair. "Oh, it's Zach and… some guy." Jett's words were so full of hatred that Derreck's anger immediately melted away. Zach and some guy hadn't met a snarky bitch like

Jett before. There was no need for Derreck to go to jail.

The one who was obviously Zach let his gaze slide down Jett's body. "Flannel. Good choice. It's best you embrace your future bear status with grace."

It was only funny because Jett had literally zero body fat and a complete inability to gain weight. Zach, on the other hand, had a small paunch and looked sturdy—like he was one missed gym trip away from full-blown weight gain. Derreck would know. He was the same.

Before Jett could claw the guy's eyes out, Kirill slipped between them. "Which is... oh, it's trash," Kirill muttered under his breath, making it harder for Derreck to keep his composure. "Tim. Zach. What can I help you with?"

Tim and Zach took turns looking at the three of them before Tim finally answered. "May we speak with you alone?" His soft voice took Derreck by surprise. The pair looked so much alike that Derreck expected equal amounts of bitchiness.

Kirill didn't seem moved by the nicer tone. "There's nothing you can say to me that can't be said in front of my husbands."

Derreck fought to keep his eyes locked on their visitors. The sound of that title weakened his knees.

Derreck hadn't realized how badly he wanted that until it was out there.

A deep line appeared between Zach's eyebrows. "Three people can't be married. That's not legal."

Kirill snorted. "You know my family. We're not real concerned with the legality of things. There's nothing Zander can't achieve if his family wants it badly enough. I wanted these men. Zander made it happen."

"You never offered that to us," Zach said, sounding petulant.

"We need a place to stay," Tim said fast, as if trying to cut off Zach before things got out of hand.

Kirill made a dismissive gesture. "Come back next week and meet the new owners. Maybe they'll be more than happy to let you suck dick in exchange for a roof over your heads."

Zach looked done.

Tim seemed a bit more willing to keep trying. "You're married and moving away. Where are you going?"

"To Vegas. With us. His husbands," Jett said, obviously relishing the reminder.

Tim honestly looked crushed. "I can't believe this. I don't believe it. How can you move on from us?"

"Okay," Jett said, losing patience. He waved Kirill and Derreck back toward the kitchen before focusing on Tim. "Look, sweetie. You're adorable and seem sweet, but also a little dumb. No offense. You two had your chance. That's over now. Kirill is off the market, so don't be pathetic." He shut the door in their faces without giving them a chance to respond. After locking the door against them, he turned back Kirill and Derreck's way. "Damn, baby. I love you and think you're one the smartest people I've ever met, but what the fuck? How did you end up with the racist bubblemint twins?"

A sexy chuckle rumbled from Kirill. "It was a moment of blind stupidity. If it makes you feel better, Zander hates them too."

That actually didn't make Derreck feel a little better. Plus, Jett was toeing the floor, looking shy and sweet—like they were about to have some of that good kitchen sex. Jett tucked a strand of dark hair behind his ear when it came loose from his bandanna.

"Um, did you mean what you said about Zander having a way for the three of us to be married?"

Derreck's gaze moved between the two of them. He held his breath. Kirill's mouth lifted in one corner in a sexy smirk. "Yes. Zander's bodyguards,

Pytor and Yaro, are part of a three-person marriage. They have a husband named Legend. I don't know the details and I imagine their marriage isn't recognized by law, but they share a last name and equal rights to one another's property. It's a marriage in their hearts."

Derreck didn't know why, but he had a hard time imagining the behemoth who escorted Derreck to see Zander that day having two husbands. Right now, that wasn't the issue, though. He was too enthralled with what was currently happening in their relationship.

Kirill looked between them. He licked his lips, looking a little nervous. "Do you think that's something you two would want?"

"I don't think. I know." The words burst from Derreck without warning. Having Kirill refer to him as his husband had broken Derreck's brain. Now he couldn't stop thinking about owning that title.

"Me too," Jett said, sounding every bit as firm. "I've never been one to care too much about what other people think. There might be some people who think we're crazy, but I want this." His gaze moved between Derreck and Kirill. "I want to tell people we're married. I need to know this is permanent."

"I need that too," Kirill said, pulling Derreck's gaze his way.

The truth settled over Derreck like a warm blanket. They were alike in every way. The three of them, they had been abandoned, beaten down, and arisen from the ashes of a previous life. Together, they were strong and whole. Three parts of the same soul. Derreck moved closer, reaching for both men. They hugged each other. Their foreheads touched. With their eyes closed, they soaked in the strength they fed one another.

"My husbands. I like that." Derreck swore saying the words made them real. That title had nothing to do with the laws of man or society. It was them. Wherever they were, they were home as long as they were together. He couldn't wait for the world to see what he had gained in them. They had found their happiness together. They had found their forever home.

Please consider clicking this link and leaving a review, https://www.amazon.com/review/create-review?asin=B085HL63BZ. Reviews really help with a book's visibility, which ensures I can continue writing. Thank you, Charity.

ABOUT THE AUTHOR

Charity Parkerson is an award winning and multi-published author with several companies. Born with no filter from her brain to her mouth, she decided to take this odd quirk and insert it in her characters.

*Eight-time Readers' Favorite Award Winner
    *2015 Passionate Plume Award Finalist
    *2013 Reviewers' Choice Award Winner
    *2012 ARRA Finalist for Favorite Paranormal Romance
    *Five-time winner of The Mistress of the Darkpath

Connect with her online:

—Sign up for my newsletter: http://bit.ly/CharityNews
    —Join my readers' group on Facebook: http://bit.ly/CharitysTribe
    —Website: charityparkerson.com

—Facebook:
facebook.com/authorCharityParkerson
facebook.com/TheMenofSin
—Twitter: twitter.com/CharityParkerso
—Instagram: Instagram.com/sinnerauthor